THE DAUGHTER'S WINTER MIRACLE

The Victorian Love Sagas
Book 1

Annie Brown

Contents

Title: The Daughter's Winter Miracle — Annie Brown

Copyright © 2023 Annie Brown

Chapter 1

"Santa Claus doesn't visit naughty children," the vexed mother screamed at her daughter, Clara, and stared at her. Esther's big, wide, dark eyes burned punishment into the young girl's soul.

Esther loomed over the child like a monster, that would bring Clara nightmares tonight. Her mother's closeness made the young girl cringe and shake with fear, whilst she sat cowering in the corner of the room. Clara struggled to comprehend her mother's screaming and deemed it unnecessary most of the time.

"He doesn't visit children who don't look after their things," she said, as she stamped on Clara's treasured doll.

Clara flinched as her mother's foot hit the porcelain head with the tight blonde curls. She started to cry as she watched it break into tiny pieces. It was her favourite gift from her father, and it broke her heart to see the doll was beyond repair. "I hate you, and I wish you weren't my mother!"

Clara screwed her eyes shut tight, hoping to not see Esther standing over her and raising her hand. The young girl's body tensed as she waited for the pain to hit. She whispered, "please don't hit me, mama, please don't." She expected another sting from her mother's hand, but there was nothing. The heavy footsteps walked away and the bedroom door slammed shut.

After sitting perfectly still for what seemed like hours, she prised one eye open. Seeing no movement, she opened the other. Clara un-furled herself, put her hands to the floor to balance her tiny frame, and stood up. She wiped her red eyes with the back of her hand and, mustered the strength to sit on her windowsill and take her thoughts to the snow outside.

Clara rested on the cold, hard windowsill of her bedroom. She could feel the Christmas spirit beckoning from the streets outside as she looked through her window. The young child watched the heavy snow falling, reflected against the oil lights and candles shining in the other houses. The bright, white, fluffy flakes of snow fell onto the ground and dressed the gardens and streets with a thick white carpet. Christmas had arrived.

Sitting with her thumb in her mouth, she longed to play outside with the other children. Clara wanted nothing more than to feel as happy as they looked and, assumed they came from happy families who were looking forward to Christmas day. The thought of love and happiness whilst opening Christmas gifts played heavily on her heart and brought a smile to her face. But it was something she would never have.

How could she go through another Christmas feeling lonely, battered, and bruised? She knew her mother loved her deep down. It's just a shame that she didn't show it and was emotionally absent all the time. Instead of caring for her daughter, as a mother should, Esther chose to berate her daughter for any reason she could think of.

Clara didn't want any Christmas presents. Instead, she prayed for a mother who would hold her tight, read stories, and sing nursery rhymes. She wanted her mother to be like her friends' parents. *I wish Christmas was fun and magical.* Clara sat watching the world go by. Her hand reached for her face and fingered the newly formed bruise on her cheekbone. Inside, she winced with pain and a teardrop formed in the corner of her eye. It came from her mother's back hand because she was playing with her toys too loudly and Esther had a headache. Something else Clara got the blame for.

When I grow up, I will love my children and my husband will adore me. I will never hit my children like mama hits me. The young, wistful, curly-haired child dreamt of the years to come. A loving husband and children running around at her feet. She imagined the candles lit at Christmas time and the gentle murmurs of Christmas carols being sung around the fire. Clara craved to hear laughter ringing through her home and it was these mature, fantastical dreams that kept her going..

Clara was not excited about the Christmas that was upon her this year. *I'd prefer a poor but loving family over a wealthy mother who despises me.*

"Clara!" No sooner had her mother left her bedroom when she was being shouted at again. "Get down these stairs now!"

It filled Clara with dread. She eased herself off the window sill, walked out of her bedroom, and slammed the door. "What have I done now?" she said, stomping down the stairs. Before she could stop herself, the young, scared child knew she shouldn't have answered back. It sent Esther into even more of a rage.

"How dare you talk to me like that you little– You left your black shoes in the entrance hall and I tripped over them."

It was a habit that drove Esther mad, but her daughter never learned the lesson. She hoped her mother would think twice about hitting her and retreat into the darkness.

Standing with her hands on her hips, her bony fingers visible on her dress, she stared at her daughter.

Clara knew better than to ignore Esther. She tentatively stood up, picked up her tiny shoes, paired them together and placed them toes facing the wall.

"How many times have I told you to tidy your shoes up?"

Clara stood staring at her mother and felt herself shaking inside. The shimmer of the Christmas tree, in the sitting room behind the wretched woman, provided a much needed warm glow to the cold atmosphere.

George, Clara's father, was in his study writing a letter when the shouting interrupted his concentration. He slammed his pen down on the desk, which then splattered ink across the cream paper. He sighed heavily expelling air through his thick pink lips. Shaking his head at the sight of tiny black dots of ink like little ants crawling across his words, he stood up. Pushing his chair back, he walked to the hallway to see what the fuss was about. "Why are you shouting?" He stood firm in the doorway with his hands on his hips. He stared at his wife waiting for an answer.

"What's the fuss about? Is it not obvious to you? I am sick of the wretched child leaving her shoes in the way. I'm convinced she does it on purpose to make me trip over them."

George smiled at his daughter. "Clara, go to your room sweet-heart," he said softly.

"Yes, papa." Clara walked back up the stairs, smiling to herself. She stepped into her room, then got into bed fully clothed and pulled the sheets and blankets right up to her chin. It made her feel safe and protected from the shouting coming from downstairs. It always fascinated her how her parents didn't think she could hear anything.

"Do you not think just for one Christmas you could be nice to her? It's not Clara's fault you have had another drink. You are always taking your foul mood out on her." George stormed off leaving Esther alone and walked upstairs to his bedroom. The married couple had not shared a room together, let alone a bed, since the death of their second child, Henry, six years ago.

He pushed the door closed and walked over to his bed. He got on his knees and looked under the bed towards the headboard. He extended his arm under the bed frame, blindly searching until he came across the box. George pulled out a gift that was wrapped and finished with a red bow and, the thought of his daughter receiving it filled his heart with joy.

The week before, Clara's father had been to Whiteley's department store. Esther was unconscious for the whole day after consuming too much brandy. She wanted to drown her sorrows and forget about the fateful day she went into labour and, gave birth to her dead son. George dreaded the anniversary too, but chose not to drown his sorrows or take his anger and grief out on his wife or child. Instead, he poured more love into Clara and tried as best as he could to look after Esther.

He stood up, dusted himself down, and made his way over to Clara's bedroom. He knocked quietly and opened the door, holding one arm behind his back, which held the gift. "Clara? There you are," he said. George didn't want to give his daughter the present just yet. At least not until he had given her some loving words of comfort. He always made sure his precious daughter was alright after a cruel and vicious encounter with Esther.

"Yes, papa?"

"Listen, Clara. You know your mother is not well. It's no excuse for the way she behaves, but at least you know it's not your fault." He smiled at her lovingly, hoping to take away the pain.

"I feel as though everything is my fault. I can't do anything right, she hates me. My mother has never loved me." Clara looked away from George's face so he couldn't see the tears.

George lifted his daughter's slender chin with his forefinger, turned her face towards him, and looked straight into her bright blue eyes. "No one loves you more than me," George said, smiling, as he brought the box from behind his back. "Here, this is for you."

"What is it?" Clara's eyes widened with delight.

"Shh, don't let her hear you. It's my Christmas gift from me to you. Make sure you treasure it."

Clara's eyes lit up with wonder. As she sat on top of her bed sheets, she crossed her legs and placed the box on her lap. She took hold of one end of the bow and pulled it until the red ribbon fell to the side of the gift. She bit her lip with her top teeth, then as she unwrapped the paper, she gasped with joy.

"Be careful with it now," George said.

Clara opened up the lid, and the music box played a simple yet beautiful melody. The tiny mirror on the lid reflected onto Clara's face making her cheeks glow.

"Papa, it's beautiful."

"For you, Clara, to find happiness when you're up here alone. You can sit in your room, open the lid, and listen to the music playing. It will bring a smile to your face - like you have now. Keep it safe under your bed and don't let your mother see it."

"I won't, papa, I promise." Clara flung her arms around her father's neck, as George looked over her shoulder and squeezed her tight.

His eyes watered, and he desperately wanted to take all her pain away. "Let me read you a bedtime story."

Clara let go of her father, jumped off the bed, and headed towards her books. She picked out her favourite, Alice's Adventures in Wonderland.

As George turned the last page and read the final sentence, he looked at Clara and noticed she had fallen asleep. Her soft, gentle, and fragile features shone in the candlelight. It was too late to disturb her now to ask her to change into her nightdress, so he pulled the covers up under her chin and kissed her on the forehead. "Goodnight my sweetheart," he whispered. Then he stood up and went over to her bedroom window. George looked outside and noticed a young girl singing Christmas carols outside, the snowflakes falling on her head.

How very festive, I wonder if the poor girl is cold? George went downstairs and opened the front door. "Happy Christmas, here you are." George reached out his hand and passed the girl a penny and a mince pie from the kitchen. The young girl's eyes widened and a smile spread across her face. "Thank you mister, and a happy Christmas to you too," she skipped away, the hem of her tattered and torn coat flapping in the breeze.

George closed the door to shut out the snow and darkness, leaving the oil lamp on to light the young girl's way. *Dear, oh dear, the poor girl is probably homeless.*

George sighed, then walked through to the library where he saw Esther asleep by the fire. Her hand held a crystal glass with a drop of amber liquid visible at the bottom. George rolled his eyes, shook his head, and went to bed.

Chapter 2

"Please don't, Oscar!" Alice said in a scared voice. The woman's wide eyes met her husband's gaze across the kitchen. Her arthritic, crooked hands visibly shaking. Slowly, she backed into the corner of the room next to the fireplace. She cowered down on her knees with nowhere to go. The fire was roaring and hot, but to Alice, it still felt cold inside the house on a wet, bleak, and miserable December day.

The sound of children's voices singing carols outside brought a moment of distraction from the trembling fear she felt inside. "Please, don't, I'm begging you. Listen to the children outside, it's meant to be a time for happiness."

"Happiness? How am I meant to be happy when I can't even feed my wife and son?"

Alice didn't have the heart to tell him that if he stopped drinking himself into an unconscious stupor, maybe they could afford a loaf of bread. Pigs trotters for a meaty broth to put some skin on their bones felt an impossibility. "I'm sorry no one has paid you today. But we're not the only ones."

Oscar snarled and bared his teeth at his wife. It was a sorry sight. "Do you think I care about anybody else?"

Alice shook her head vigorously and looked away quickly. She didn't want to meet his eyes again. "We can—we can—me and Jack, well, we can always go around the posh houses and see if they want to buy anything from you." Alice crossed her fingers behind her back. For a moment, everything seemed quiet whilst Oscar raised his eyebrows. Alice held her breath.

"Won't work. They don't like us, them posh folk. Too busy gallivanting around their private gardens and singing around the piano."

"Exactly—exactly. They need, they need—" Alice's mind ran through the various needs and wants that houses fit for royalty might desire.

"I'm waiting."

"Well, they always need new furniture, them lot. Perhaps a new plump, upholstered, mahogany seat?"

"You're being ridiculous, they don't want nowt from me."

Alice slowly stood up. "I think your seats are beautiful. Perhaps we could have one in here." Her hopes of pacifying Oscar to avoid more bruises were quickly fading.

"You're hopeless, you are. You never come up with proper suggestions. Ones that would bring us in more money."

Alice started to bite her fingernails. She realised she was out of time. "Why don't you sit down by the fire, and I'll bring you a drink," she quickly made her way to the kitchen, skirting past her husband.

"A drink? What about supper?" Oscar's words went unheard.

Alice slammed the ladle down on the wooden table in the kitchen. Her knuckles turned white and tears started to trickle down her face. She couldn't take anymore. The emotionally battered woman closed her eyes and took a deep breath. "Food? Food? You've got to be kidding me? We haven't seen any decent food in weeks. And all because you'd rather drink yourself into a stupor than feed your family." She knew she'd said too much.

Oscar stood up. His heavy frame stomped towards his wife. "I haven't got a proper family. Our Matilda's dead! Our little girl isn't even here this winter."

"Ask yourself why, Oscar. Why isn't she here? Because you killed her that's why! It's not enough for you that I lied to the police to save you from being arrested. I shouldn't have done it though, then perhaps it would have meant me and Jack could sleep at night, instead of worrying ourselves stupid over what you're going to do to us every day."

"How dare you! Come here, or I'll—"

Alice circled the kitchen table. "Or you'll what? Beat me up black and blue, then say I fell again? There's only so many times you can say that without it sounding suspicious, and you're well over your quota."

"You little—"

"Go on, say it Oscar. Then beat us both up until you're happy."

"It's not my fault she died, you know," Oscar's lips quivered. "You're the one that left her by the fire."

"Aye, and I asked you to look after her. You couldn't do something so simple, could you? Your precious grog was more important than our little girl!"

Oscar launched himself across the kitchen table, and Alice had nowhere to go. He grabbed hold of her, then pulled his belt from his waist and raised it above his head. Meanwhile, young Jack sat at the top of the stairs weeping.

Chapter 3

J ack had shifted from the stairs to his bed and hid under the blankets. The ramshackle of a bed, with its worn bed sheets and blankets, was the only place where he felt warm and safe. "Please don't hurt ma, please don't hurt her." His whispers sounded loud in the stillness of the room. *I hope he hasn't heard me.* Dressed in striped pyjamas with holes in the elbows and knees, his young body froze at the sound of footsteps. He held his breath and felt like his chest was going to explode if he didn't breathe out soon.

Alice fell to the floor after Oscar had finished. She watched the Christmas snow falling outside, then saw her husband unconscious on the stone floor from drinking too much.

The young mother struggled to stand. She reached out for the upturned chair to gain some balance to pull herself up. The beaten woman tiptoed up the stairs, one step at a time. Her hand gripped the worm-holed banister as she took a glance back at the body on the floor and prayed to God he wouldn't wake up. She had to reach her son.

"Jack, Jack, wake up," Alice said in a whisper. She shook her son gently and crawled into the tiny bed next to him under the covers. She let out a deep breath, closed her eyes, and made the sign of the cross on her forehead and chest. *In the name of the Father, and of the Son, and of the Holy Spirit. Amen.*

"Yes, ma, I'm awake," he whispered.

"Jack, listen to me, you cannot stay here. As soon as it becomes light, you must run away as far as possible to the City of London and find your Uncle Cecil. He will look after you."

Jack frowned, his eyes screwed shut.

"Please, Jack, don't be scared," she said.

The young boy looked at his mother searching for an explanation. Not that he needed it.

"But what will you do? Are you not coming with me?"

"I can't. I need to stay here and distract your father from coming after you."

Jack looked at his mother with tears in his eyes. "But I don't want to leave you here."

"You have to, Jack. You have no choice. I will not have you here whilst your father continues like this. Trust me, this is for the best." Alice tried not to sound emotional, so he couldn't see her upset. She pulled him into her chest and hugged him."

"I don't know my Uncle Cecil, how will I find him? I'm too scared."

"Listen to me. He works as a fabric merchant helping posh people and the theatres with suits and costumes. Find him, and tell him I told you to stay with him until I can come to you when it's safe."

Jack flung his spindly arms around Alice.

"Don't be scared, Jack. I will sleep with you tonight and we'll get you ready at dawn."

A few hours later the light started to shine through the window - Alice was already gathering a few things together for Jack's journey. She filled his coat pockets with pieces of fruit that had seen better days. "Jack, come here quickly before your father wakes up." She beckoned the boy out of bed and dressed him in the warmest of clothes he had. "Here, put these on." Alice clothed him in an old shirt, two jumpers, trousers, socks, and a pair of old boots.

"I have put two apples and oranges in your pockets," she said as she put on his hat and tied his threadbare scarf around his neck.

This Christmas would be unlike any other. There would be no gifts or food on the table, and Jack wouldn't be with his family. Alice would have no one to sing Christmas carols to at night. The thought of it brought her to tears and, she tried to hide her emotions so Jack wouldn't see her upset.

"Here, take this crown and keep it in your pocket. Only use it if you have to, and make it last."

Jack had never seen such a shiny coin before. His eyes were wide with delight. "Ma, where did you get this from?"

"I saved it knowing this day would come. Now go." Alice hugged Jack as she winced with pain from her cuts and bruises. "I love you, Jack."

"I love you too, ma."

Quietly, Jack tiptoed down the stairs, sneaking past his unconscious father. The creaking door caused his face to tighten. After glancing over at Oscar and checking he was still asleep, Jack closed the door. He turned around to face the cold and hunched his shoulders against the intrepid weather. Flecks of soft snow glued to his scarf and hat. After looking from side to side, to make sure no one saw him, he took a deep breath and ran down the street as fast as possible.

Chapter 4

"Where have you been? I've been waiting hours for you both. I couldn't find you anywhere and supper is now ruined! I put in so much effort cooking your favourite meal." Esther slumped on the chair and rested her chin on her hand. She gazed towards the floor.

George gulped and silently let out a breath through his nose. He tentatively walked towards his wife. "I'm sorry," he said, reaching for her hand.

Esther brushed him away.

"Clara and I went shopping to buy you a Christmas gift. We thought it would make you happy. We both think you will like it, don't we, Clara?" He turned around and looked at his daughter, raising his eyebrows as confirmation.

"Yes, yes, we do." Clara stood behind her father's back. All she wanted to do was stick pins in her mother's eyes.

"That's very kind of you," she said, looking up at her family. "Supper won't be hot though."

Clara could do nothing but roll her eyes at her mother's ungratefulness.

George tentatively passed the box to his wife.

Esther took the box from George and rested it on her lap. The box was bright and stood out against the dull, brown fabric of her dress. She unfastened the bow with her long, spindly fingers and George thought he saw a glimmer of excitement in her eyes.

Clara held her breath, waiting for her mother to speak.

"Thank you," she said, as she placed it around her neck. She tied the scarf delicately, then stood up and twirled around. She stroked the fabric and the ends of the silk garment flapped in the air.

"So you like it then, mama?" Clara frowned and waited for her mother's approval again.

"I just said so, didn't I? What do you want? Praise?" Esther walked past them both, and Clara's head dropped to the floor.

"I thought we were doing the right thing papa."

George pursed his lips together and rubbed the back of his neck. "I think Clara, we have to remember it's this time of year when Henry died. Your mother finds it hard to deal with."

"She's always angry and upset. I don't think she will ever be happy." Clara rubbed her eyes and walked away, leaving a bereft George behind on his own in the drawing room.

"Where do you think you're going?" Esther bellowed up the stairs after her daughter.

"I'm not hungry."

"You will get down these stairs now and come and eat supper. It might be cold, but that doesn't mean you will waste it."

Clara knew better than to ignore her. After what had been an exciting afternoon with her papa, listening to Christmas carols on the streets and looking through the decorated windows, she gazed down and walked down the stairs slowly with her hands loosely behind her back. Her stomach quivered as she walked past her mother into the dining room.

"That's better. Now go and sit next to your father."

The fire in the dining room was roaring and felt welcoming and George imagined that one year, life would be back to normal. The same as it was before young Henry took his last breath. His right knee bounced under the table and he drew in a silent breath. "How has your afternoon been, Esther?" George sensed his wife had been drinking.

"It's not been the happiest."

For a moment, George felt a pang in his heart.

"I have been waiting for you to come back home for hours. Do you think that's how I want to spend my time?"

"I'm sorry, but I did tell you where we were going. I thought it would be a nice surprise buying you a Christmas gift." He noticed that Esther seemed to relax a little.

The disturbing clatter as Clara's knife clashed with the porcelain plate made everyone jump. The gravy on her plate splashed onto her clean dress. She looked up slowly, then glanced at her father, looking to be rescued from her mother's wrath.

Esther slammed her knife and fork down on her plate in unison and stood up. She walked over to her daughter and looked down at her, pointing a finger close to her face. "I will not have bad table manners in this house, Clara. How many times have I told you to concentrate whilst you are eating your dinner and, to not listen to what your father and I are talking about?"

"I'm sorry, mama, I didn't mean to do it, honest."

"You naughty child, get up to your room immediately." Esther lifted her hand in the air, but stopped herself from hitting her daughter when she saw the look on George's face.

George ran his hand through his hair. *Enough, I've had enough! I can't take this any longer.*

Clara ran upstairs to her bedroom. The sound of her crying made George bite his bottom lip. "Esther, just leave it," George snapped. "I'm fed up with you treating her like that, she did nothing wrong, it was an accident."

Esther went over to George and slapped him across his face. He could smell the liquor on her breath. His face knocked sideways, his cheek went red from her hand touching his skin.

"How dare you talk to me like that? Don't tell me not to chastise my daughter, she has to learn some manners."

"Our daughter," George said. "She is our daughter, Esther. I love her and will not see her get hurt. She is just an eight-year-old girl doing everything she can to avoid being shouted at by you. She's scared every day and afraid of talking to you. How would you like it if your mother had treated you like that?"

Esther's eyes watered. She blinked slowly, looked away from her husband, and sat back down in her chair.

"Stop taking your grief out on her. It's not Clara's fault that Henry died."

"What do you mean it's not her fault?" She's the one who's still alive. It should be Clara that's dead, not Henry."

Clara sat at the top of the stairs listening, visibly trembling.

"What do you mean it should be Clara that's dead? How can you be so hurtful towards your—sorry—our daughter? No wonder she fears you every time she walks through the door. She's petrified and tries to do her best because she wants your love." George turned around and looked out of the window and rubbed his forehead.

"I don't care if she wants my love, I don't have any more to give. All the love I had left my heart when Henry died." Esther turned away from her husband and rested her fist against her lips.

George sighed deeply. "I've had enough!" He said in a thick, emotion-fueled voice. He stormed out of the dining room and went after his daughter.

Esther slumped into the green upholstered and mahogany framed chair, and reached for a crystal glass from the trolley beside her. She poured herself a brandy and brought the dark-brown, silky liquid to her lips. She lit a cigarette, shrugged her shoulders, and blew smoke rings into the air. The misty-grey and smokey-blue clouds floated past the gentle glow of the Christmas lights.

"I'm so sorry you had to hear what your mother said, Clara." George wrapped his arms around his daughter. He held her close and closed his eyes against her hair.

"I know that she would rather I was dead than Henry. I haven't done anything wrong. I don't understand."

"Don't you worry," he said as he stroked her long, flowing curls. "Let's get you ready for bed and read you a story."

George stood up and followed Clara into her bedroom. He locked the door so Esther couldn't come in.

"Papa?"

"Yes?"

"I wish I didn't have a mother."

George's heart felt heavy and he wished for Clara's sake, that life was different. He knew how it felt to have parents who didn't love you. And he wished he'd acted differently all those years ago. Now, it was time to protect his only child.

Clara leaned into her father, his arm around her shoulders. She looked out of the window at the snow gently falling, as a single teardrop fell down her cheek and onto her bed clothes.

Chapter 5

"Where's Jack?" Oscar stomped up the stairs and rubbed his forehead. He hadn't shaved in days and his clothes were grey and stinking. Jack had only been gone a couple of hours when Oscar had woken up with a heavy head. He bit his lip and tried to remember what had happened the night before. "Jack! I can't manage by myself, I need you to come to work with me today."

Alice sat on the side of her bed, biting the wicks of her finger nails. Dark circles were visible under eyes.

"Where is he?" Oscar checked his son's bedroom first and, finding it empty, his heavy footsteps took him to his own room. "Where has he gone? I need him!" The hesitation in Oscar's voice was barely audible. Enough to leave Alice uncertain about his memory of hurting her.

Oscar looked toward his wife waiting for an answer.

Alice took a deep breath. "He's run away, Oscar. I don't think he's coming back."

"There will be trouble if that boy doesn't come back!"

"I think that's why he left, he was scared. He heard the shouting last night and left before I woke up."

Oscar ran his hands through his hair. "If I hear you have any part to play in this, I'll—"

"You'll what? Beat me black and blue like you did last night? One day you won't stop and I'll be dead." Alice looked away sharply.

Oscar cracked his knuckles, turned around, walked out, and slammed the door.

Alice let out a deep, heavy breath.

"I'll find him, you'll see!" Oscar shouted behind him.

His voice made Alice jump. She dropped her head, closed her eyes, and prayed that Jack was far enough away for his father not to find him.

Chapter 6

The young boy hadn't travelled very far. He found a ginnel to shelter for the night. Sitting on the cold, frozen ground beneath him, he started to cry. He searched his pocket for the penny the kind man gave him for singing a Christmas carol. That and the shiny crown his ma had given him, wouldn't get him very far.

Jack looked down towards his feet and wriggled his toes to reveal the sole coming away from his left shoe. His foot felt wet and cold and his small fingers felt for the hole between boot and sole. *That's why my socks are wet, no wonder my toes feel frozen. I'm going to have to find my Uncle Cecil, it can't be that hard. Then I can sit in front of a warm fire and dry out. Maybe he will give me something to eat.* Jack closed his eyes and imagined an open fire with a comfortable armchair either side. A beautifully decorated Christmas tree caught his eye in the corner of the room. He imagined his uncle sitting in the chair opposite him with a warm, welcoming face, a grey beard, and a big smile. *I hope he's nothing like my father. When I've found him, maybe he will send for ma.* He brought his knees up to his chest and wrapped his arms around them. His bottom lip started to quiver.

"My, my, young Jack. What are you doing out in this freezing weather on your own?"

Jack opened his eyes and stared at the old, greying woman with a basket over her arm. He couldn't take his gaze away from the loaf of bread, vegetables, and turkey, all poking out of the top of the basket. His mouth began to water.

"Jack, don't be scared, what's happened? It's not like you not to be at school or hanging around your ma's ankles."

"I'm not allowed to say." Jack pierced his lips, and he closed his eyes, letting his head fall to his knees again.

"Maybe I can help. Has something happened to your ma and pa? Do you want me to take you home?"

"No! Sorry, I didn't mean to shout. No, thank you, Mrs Kipling, I will be fine."

The old woman frowned. She couldn't let him stay on the snowy streets.

Jack glanced at the plump woman with chestnut brown curly hair and a rosy round face. He could feel the warmth from her friendly features emulating him.

Mrs Kipling looked at the young child as she lifted the heavy basket of groceries further up her arm with a heave. She noticed the glint in Jack's eyes when she saw him staring at the food. "Are you hungry, son? When was the last time you ate?"

Jack's loud, grumbling stomach at the thought of food answered for him.

Mrs Kipling sighed at the sight of the young lad in front of her. "Jack, you're coming home with me and you can tell me all about it."

"But—"

"No buts about it, come on. We need to get you warm before you freeze to death. I don't want your ma and pa burying you at Christmas time."

"I don't mean to cause my ma any trouble, Missus'. I can make my own way home."

"I think you're lying, Jack. I know your mother too well to believe that she would leave you out in the freezing cold. You'll get sick and she can't afford a doctor."

Jack twisted his mouth to the side. "Promise you won't tell anyone?"

"Tell them what?"

"Just promise."

"Okay, I promise, as long as you don't lie to me." Her hand gripped the young boy's hand.

"My ma has sent me to find my Uncle Cecil."

"What made her do that?"

Jack shrugged his shoulders.

"Ouch," she whispered, feeling the tug on her arthritic knees as she squatted down beside the young boy. "Does this have anything to do with your pa?"

Jack pierced his lips together. "Promise you won't say anything."

"I won't Jack, I've already said that. But I can't help you if I don't know."

"He hurt my ma last night. I overheard everything from the top of the stairs, then rushed to my room and hid under the covers."

"And then what happened?"

"Ma came upstairs after a while. There were a few bruises on her face. Her eye was red and her dress was torn. She told me I couldn't stay anymore and, that I should leave at dawn to find Uncle Cecil."

"Where is your Uncle?"

"The City of London, Missus'."

"The City of London? That's at least another three days of walking. Where are you going to sleep?"

"I'm hoping to find some shelter along the way."

The old woman sighed, resigned. How could she possibly leave a young child she knew out on the freezing, wintry streets? "Come home with me, Jack. I can't leave you out in the cold this Christmas. I will ask Ethan to take you as far as he can in his rented carriage a couple of days after Christmas. That will save your feet and stop you dying from the cold. And you will have Christmas with us." Betty brimmed with pride as the tiny red veins in her cheeks showed against the cold weather.

"Thank you."

She held out her hand and Jack grabbed hold of it, pulling himself up. He checked his pockets to make sure his rich belongings had not fallen out, then followed Betty back to her house.

"You're safe with me now, son. Let's get you back to our house and work out what you will do."

Jack trekked the cobbled streets through the packed, slippy snow, hoping he hadn't said too much.

Chapter 7

George knocked on Clara's bedroom door. He put his ear to the wood when he didn't hear a sound and knocked again. "Clara?" He turned the black door knob and stepped inside expecting his daughter to be in her room playing. "Clara?" George looked around the young girl's bedroom and frowned. *How odd, where is she?*

He hurried down the stairs. "Clara? Clara? Where are you?"

"Do you have to shout so loud?" Esther rubbed her forehead and screwed her eyes closed.

"It's not my fault you drank too much. I'm more concerned with where Clara is than your self-inflicted headache!" George whooshed past his wife and started searching the house. He walked to the drawing room where he had left his wife drinking the night before. George wished his wife would be like how she was before Henry's death. Kind, caring, loving, and nurturing her family was never a task or chore. Now, it appeared she hated those closest to her.

His daughter being up and dressed so early was unusual, especially with the heavy snow outside. She wasn't keen on the cold weather, preferring instead to be curled up by the fire reading a book.

"Margaret, have you seen Clara?" he asked the housekeeper.

"I'm sorry, Mr Cavendish, I haven't." The housekeeper wiped her hands on her apron leaving floury imprints on the material. "Maybe she's next door with William and Philip. She likes helping them muck out the stables."

"Yes, you're right. I'll get my coat and boots and walk over there."

"If I find her, I'll come for you." Margaret hurried up the stairs to check every bedroom.

Esther stood in the hallway rolling her eyes at the commotion. "For heaven's sake, she is probably just out somewhere!"

"I'm glad you're so concerned. It's more likely she has run away from you."

Esther rolled her eyes and walked up stairs towards her bedroom. "I'm going to lie down. Margaret, don't allow anyone to disturb me."

George clenched his fists by his side and felt his chest rise and fall with each heavy breath. He grabbed his jacket and fastened the buttons quickly, then stepped outside into the snow. It was only after he reached the end of the drive, he realised he was still in his slippers. "Claaara? Claaara?" He looked around, hoping to see his daughter happily playing in the festive weather.

"Do you think you'll be able to manage this weather on your own? I'm scared for you," Philip said.

Clara looked at him with dark eyes. "If you knew what she was like, you would have packed your bag as well. I don't want her to be my mama anymore."

"But, Clara, you're only eight, neither of us are old enough to be leaving home."

"I thought you would come with me. I thought we were friends." Clara's bottom lip protruded.

"I still am your best friend. It's just that I don't want to leave home. I love my ma and pa."

"Hmm, I wish mine would love me."

"That's not fair, your pa loves you." Philip played with a single strand of hay whilst Clara leant against him for warmth.

"Yes, I suppose."

"I think you should go home. It will be Christmas day soon."

Clara let out a deep sigh. Fun and happiness in the young girl's life didn't happen very often. "If you're not coming with me, I'm going to go now." Without saying another word, she picked up her bag, her body leaning to one side to keep the bag off the ground, and started walking away.

"What's in there? It looks heavy. Have you packed your toys?"

Clara's cheeks turned pink. "Mostly clothes, and a couple of books and one toy."

"Haha, you won't be needing those on the streets."

Clara walked off with tears in her eyes feeling heartbroken and lonely.

Philip watched Clara walk away. He hoped she would change her mind and walk back towards him, but she kept on going and got further away into the distance. He bit his bottom lip and started to run.

George ran into the stables to look for his daughter. He ran past the horses and bales of hay hoping to find her with her friend. Philip met him running in the opposite direction.

"Philip, Philip, have you seen Clara?"

"Oh, it's you, Mr Cavendish. Yes, she has run away from home, I've just seen her leave with a bag."

"Why didn't you stop her?"

"I tried to, but she told me she didn't want to live with her ma anymore. I'm about to run after her."

"Which way did she go?"

Philip pointed straight ahead up the middle of the tree lined drive. "That way. Do you want me to come?"

"No, you wait here in case she comes back. I'm going after her." George ran as fast as he could down the slippery drive. Occasionally, his feet would slide apart, struggling to maintain their balance. "Clara, Clara!"

There was no sign of the young girl and feeling breathless and the panic rise in his throat, he started to think the worst. *I can't have her running away, what if I never see her again? She's never done this before.* George rubbed the inside collar of his coat and his breathing quickened. Tears started to form in the father's eyes when he thought about the Christmas gift that he bought her. The worry was clear from his watery gaze when he couldn't imagine a day without his beautiful, precious daughter beside him. "Claaara? Claaara?"

"What's papa doing running up the drive? If Philip has told him I've run away—" The runaway hid behind an enormous oak tree and pursed her lips together. Resting her head against the rough bark, she closed her eyes. *I love you papa, I don't know what to do.* She kept as quiet as possible as George ran past the tree she was hiding behind.

A flutter in George's stomach made him stop, and turn around on the spot. He looked carefully for his daughter's dark green coat. Something she wouldn't be without in this weather. He squinted and looked around slowly and saw something flapping behind the tree. He walked forward and tilted his head to the side to try and get a look at what had caught his eye.

Clara felt like she had been holding her breath for minutes. Her lips remained pursed together as she heard her father's footsteps crunching in the snow.

George's slippers were soaked wet through but he didn't care. All he wanted was his daughter.

"Clara?" He reached out and touched the back of her shoulder.

"Papa." She spun around and burst into tears.

George grabbed hold of his her and held her close to his chest whilst she sobbed.

"I'm sorry, papa. I didn't know what to do. I wanted to run away and never come back. Mama hates me." Clara's shoulders shook up and down.

"Shh, there, there. Let's get you home." George guided his daughter with her bag back to the house. He was uncertain of his next move, but knew he had to stop her pain. He couldn't stand losing another child.

He came to the only drastic solution he could think of, because his wife's despicable behaviour called for desperate measures.

Chapter 8

The snowflakes fell softly onto the ground on Christmas Eve. Jack tiptoed to look out of the window at children having fun outside. He instinctively ducked as they threw a snowball towards the glass. The young boy who had thrown it ran up to the windowpane and placed both hands on it, fingers spread-eagled, then laughed and ran away. The fun emanating from the children made Jack more certain it was the life he wanted.

Perhaps I'll have a family like this someday. He turned around from the window and noticed Mrs Kipling's children were playing in front of the fire. *This place is no bigger than ma and pa's house, so where do all the children sleep?* He stood looking at the siblings tormenting each other and having fun, not knowing what to do or how to join in. Two children looked up at him, smiled, then went back to their marbles.

Betty walked through to the kitchen where her husband was sitting having a cup of tea. "I've brought the young lad up from the farm home with me." She heaved her heavy basket from the crook of her arm, and let it drop onto the large wooden kitchen table. It was worn with cracks and scratches with six odd chairs placed around it.

The weight of the basket landed with a thud, sending a couple of splashes of hot tea from her husband's mug onto the table, soaking into the wood. Ethan wiped the residue away with his forearm. "What young lad?"

"You know, Jack, from the farm. I found him on the streets, the poor, young soul. It looked like he was about to meet his death in that weather." She shivered and rubbed her hands over the stove. "He told me his mother had asked him to run away and find his Uncle Cecil in the City of London."

"Why has his ma made him leave?" Ethan slurped his tea.

"I don't know. Maybe things have got worse between her and Oscar. I said he could stay here with us for Christmas, then you will take him as far as possible towards London."

"Aye, that's no problem, my love. Another mouth to feed this time of year won't make a difference."

"I love you, Mr Kipling," she said, as she walked over to him and planted a kiss on his lips.

"Come here," he said, grabbing his wife around the waist and spinning around. "Do you think we should give him a stocking? Make him feel welcome?"

"That's no problem to me. I've plenty of those holey things spare. A little darning will keep the fruit and coal from falling out."

Both Mr and Mrs Kipling walked through to the living room and the scene in front of them brought smiles to their faces.

"Children, it's Christmas time and Jack will be staying with us for a few nights." Betty walked over to the tattered armchair by the fire and sunk her heavy frame into it. She leaned forward and rubbed her hands in front of the flames. The heat made her cheeks flush pink.

Jack looked around at the Kipling family and smiled shyly.

"Jack is going to share your bed, Oliver. Make sure you don't roll on top of him in the night."

The other children laughed at their sibling. Jack looked on and smiled at the relaxed humour.

"Whilst your ma makes some soup and bread for supper, someone sing me a Christmas song."

Jack tentatively looked around whilst the Kipling children covered their mouths and giggled quietly.

"Come on, don't keep me waiting."

"Yes, Edith, don't keep papa waiting, Johnny said.

"Why is it always me? I hate singing!"

"Although you may not like it, your voice is like that of a starling, my love."

Jack glanced around, but the four children remained silent.

"Silent night, holy night!
All is calm, all is bright.
Round yon Virgin, Mother and Child.
Holy infant, so tender and mild,
Sleep in heavenly peace,
Sleep in heavenly peace..."

"My, Jack, that's good. Where did you learn that?"

"Oh, Ma used to sing to me in bed at Christmas time, sir, but this year she won't get the chance."

"Well, it's a fine voice you've got young lad, I'll give you that."

Little Jack shrugged his shoulders in response and smiled at the kind, man. He wished his father could have been like him.

"Right, children, supper time, then it's up to bed for you lot, or Santa Claus won't be visiting." Betty held her lower back, and hobbled into the kitchen. The arthritic pain in her knees wasn't getting any easier. But she brushed it off with a big grin and a heavy jaunt towards the big wooden table.

After supper, the children followed their ma up to the shared bedrooms.

"Johnny, you're the same size as Jack, lend him those pyjamas from that bottom drawer, I'm sure they're clean. If they're not, they'll do for one night."

Mr and Mrs Kipling tucked each of the children into bed. They brought the bed covers up to their chins and pressed them against the shoulders.

"Goodnight, Jack," Betty said.

"Goodnight, Missus. Thank you." Jack closed his eyes and within a couple of minutes he was snoring.

Betty looked down at him, moved closer, and kissed him on the forehead. "Where are those extra socks? The poor lad might be homeless, but he still deserves a Christmas. I don't want him to feel left out."

"Did anybody tell you that you are wonderful, my love?"

"Ethan! Shh, you made me jump. I thought I was whispering to myself."

"Come here." Ethan put his arm around his wife and kissed her on the cheek.

"Let's give the lad a Christmas to remember, hey? Who knows when he will get another one like it again?"

Chapter 9

George sat in his empire chair and crossed his legs underneath the polished, mahogany desk. He clasped his hands together, twisted his wedding ring on his finger and rested his hands in front of him. The sepia photograph of his daughter, framed in gold leaf with embossed carvings of oak leaves and acorns, sat on the far corner of his desk. It drew his mind back to when his daughter was born, a period when he was happily married to Esther and couldn't imagine his life without her. Henry hadn't yet been born and everybody was happy in the loving, welcoming home in Holly village.

Now, he couldn't imagine another day living with Esther's torrid and out of character behaviour. He had become accustomed to the grief and torment that Esther inflicted on him and he had learned how to handle it. He wasn't happy about how she acted towards him or Clara and wished life was how it used to be. But at least he could manage her outbursts.

The person he pitied the most was Clara. Such a young girl who didn't deserve the belittling and emotionally neglecting attitude from someone who was supposed to love them with all of their heart.

I must do something about this. I can't have Clara isolating herself and running away.

"Papa, are you okay?"

The sweet voice brought George's presence back into the room. When he looked up, the sight of his precious daughter brought a smile to his face.

"Clara, have you been in your bedroom all this time?" He reached out his arms, drawing Clara closer to him to sit on his knee.

Clara put her mouth to George's ear and guarded it with her hand. She whispered, "Yes, papa. I've been playing with the music box you bought me."

"That's my girl, I knew you would like it."

"Is mama asleep? I hope so."

George gulped. "Yes, she's in her bedroom having a nap."

Clara, once again put her mouth to her father's ear. "That's good."

George blinked quickly, trying to dissolve the water in his eyes. "Clara, listen. I'll be back soon."

"Where are you going?"

I need to go to the grocery store to pick something up."

"Do you have to leave me alone? I don't like it."

"Listen, I won't be long I promise, go back upstairs and shut your door and play quietly. I promise your mother will still be asleep when I get back."

Clara gave her father a kiss on the cheek, then jumped down off his knee and went to her bedroom.

It broke George's heart to see his young daughter with her bag packed. He shook his head at the memory. How can an eight-year-old girl feel so desperate?

George re-considered his options before shopping for the inevitable solution. Leaving home with his daughter would be impossible. They would be homeless, hungry, and penniless. When Esther's wealthy parents died, his wife inherited most of the estate and investments, and they were in her name.

So, he had done his research, thought carefully about the consequences, and decided there was only one option. Sniffing, then wiping his nose with his handkerchief, he then put his coat on and left the house. The general store was just a short walk away.

"Good afternoon, Mr Cavendish."

Head down and marching on, George was determined to do what he had to before second-guessing himself. He lifted his collar around his neck and ignored Mabel from Hepworth House. Trudging through the snow, he continued to hold the picture of his daughter in his mind to convince himself he was doing the right thing.

He reached the grocery store and stepped inside. "Good afternoon, Mrs Braithwaite."

"Hello, Mr Cavendish, how are you today?"

"I'm very well thank you, how are you?" George shuffled from foot to foot and looked at the wooden shelves behind Mrs Braithwaite. His eyes scanned the shelves holding food, household wares, lotions, and potions, until he could find what he was looking for.

"I'm still feeling very festive. You know what it's like when you have young children. They think Santa Claus is going to visit every day."

George had forgotten what the Christmas festivities felt like. It had been that long since his family had celebrated the festive session properly. "Your children are very lucky to have a loving mother like yourself."

"They are my children, after all," the puzzled woman said. Her eyebrows furrowing together.

"Not all mothers share that sentiment though, do they?"

"I think you might be right. I heard that a young boy from the farm had nowhere to go on Christmas Eve. His ma had made him run away. Beats me why parents don't look after their kids properly. They might not have had much money but it doesn't cost anything to love them, does it?"

"No, it doesn't," George said, thoughtfully.

"Fortunately, Mrs Kipling took him in for Christmas." The plump, friendly woman beckoned George closer to her. "Word is that his ma made him run away so he wouldn't get beaten up. Apparently his pa was a bit heavy handed. Couldn't afford a loaf of bread and took it out on his wife and son. He liked a lot of this." Mrs Braithwaite held an imaginary bottle and shook it back and forth.

"That's a shame, but very kind of Mrs Kipling to take him in."

"I suppose it is Christmas after all," she said, shuffling behind the counter.

George looked over the woman's shoulder at the shelves of produce feeling frustrated there was no sign of what he needed.

Agnes Braithwaite noticed his attention had shifted away from the conversation. "What can I get for you?"

"Just some arsenic please, Mrs Braithwaite. I can't see it on the shelves."

"You won't be able to, I keep it under the counter. Poisonous stuff that you know. I trust you'll use it sensibly? How much would you like?"

"We need to deter some rats at the back of the house."

"This will be enough then." Agnes handed over the arsenic thinking nothing more of it. She watched George leave the shop and couldn't stop looking at him. *There's definitely something not right with Mr Cavendish today.*

George looked up and down the street when he opened the shop door and, without another moment's hesitation, he left with the arsenic to go and do what he had to do.

Chapter 10

⁂

J ack had a warm glow to his cheeks. Having feasted on goose, pota-
toes, and other vegetables rescued from the cold, winter ground,
he rubbed his protruding belly whilst sat by the fire. He had ripped
the entire flesh from the bones of the goose, leaving them clean.

Mrs Kipling and her family had looked on at the young, starving
lad. Their mouths closed and their eyes wide.

"You must have been hungry, didn't you get fed at home?"

Jack shook his head. "No, pa had little money. We ate vegetable
broth and dried bread."

Mrs Kipling's eyebrows furrowed together. "Make sure you've had enough to eat. I've made you two rounds of salt meat sandwiches for your journey. I hope it will be enough until you find your uncle."

"Thank you, I've had the best Christmas ever."

Mrs Kipling brought her arms across her chest in front of her heart and tilted her head. "You're very welcome, Jack. Now, do you have everything you need for your trip to London?"

The little boy nodded with enthusiasm, but deep down inside his belly, he felt nervous about what the next few days had in store for him.

"Go on then, go and catch Mr Kipling, he's in the carriage outside waiting for you. And you be careful on those streets and stay warm, do you hear me?"

Jack nodded and smiled at the woman standing in front of him. Betty reached down and gave him a tight hug, wrapping her motherly arms around his slender frame. Jack felt his body melt and squashed against the woman's bosom. She kissed him on top of his head and said goodbye.

The Kipling children, still excited after Christmas, ran outside and waved to their new friend. Little Tom ran up to the carriage, reached up and passed Jack an apple. "This will stop you getting hungry."

"Thanks, Tom, I'll save it for later. And remember what I told you, go round the houses and sing and you'll get shiny pennies."

The young boy's eyes lit up like the pennies Jack spoke about then he ran off back inside the house to practice.

Jack gave the Kipling family one last smile and a wave. With a tear in his eye, he didn't want to say anything for fear of bursting into full blown sobs.

"Jack! Jack! Hang on." Betty hobbled over to the carriage and took hold of Jack's hand. "I hope you find him, son. We'll miss you."

"Right then, hang on lad, and let's get you on your way."

Jack bit his thumbnail. He felt nervous about what lay ahead and conflicted between worried thoughts about his ma, and moments of happiness thinking about Christmas with the Kiplings'. He held on tight, looking from left to right as they rode the cobbled streets and him and Ethan brushed snowflakes from their eyes.

After an hour of the carriage making its way along the snowy streets, Mr Kipling and Jack came to a stop just a short distance away from London.

"This is a good place for you to begin your journey."

"Thank you, sir, I don't know how I will ever repay you."

"You don't need to, just be careful and good luck."

Jack jumped off the carriage that Mr Kipling had borrowed. He still had his crown and penny and remembered the sandwiches and fruit wrapped in the bundle that Betty made him.

It was freezing cold outside, and the light of the day was fading. Jack could see the oil lights in the windows of the posh houses shining out onto the streets below and wished he was inside keeping warm. With the snow still falling and the light disappearing, he became less hopeful of finding his uncle today.

He walked the streets, oblivious, gazing at the grand houses. He had never seen such sights before and wondered who lived in them. *These houses are so big, I would get lost inside one of those.* His eyes widened with delight and his mouth opened in awe at the size of the buildings.

He walked further from the houses and found a shop, hoping it was open. He looked through the window, shielding his forehead to remove the reflection. After seeing a gentleman behind the shop counter, he opened the door and stepped inside.

"Don't come here to beg, borrow, or steal. I've had enough of people like you snatching things from me."

This can't be my uncle. Jack stood behind the counter and looked at the shopkeeper looming over him.

"What can I do for you today? A bar of soap, looking at the state of you."

"Er, no, sir."

"Well, come on then, speak up. What is it you want? I'm a very busy man!"

"Is your name Cecil?"

"What do you mean, is my name Cecil?"

Jack repeated himself. "Is your name Cecil? I'm looking for my Uncle Cecil, sir."

"No, it is not! Now, if that's all, please leave. I don't want your kind in this shop. I have standards to maintain for my customers." The candlemaker turned around and continued wrapping candles and stacking them in piles on the shelves behind him.

Jack frowned, his mouth upturned. Shrugging his shoulders, he started to think he should have stayed with his ma until she was ready to leave with him.

He continued to walk along the streets when a man and woman dressed in their fine winter clothes walked towards him. As they brushed past him, the gentleman turned to him. "Watch it, young boy," he said. "You do not touch women like that. Do you hear me?"

Jack frowned and backed away. "I—I—I'm sorry, sir. But I did nothing. I was just walking along the pavement looking for my uncle."

"Looking for your uncle?" The gentleman chuckled as he spoke. "If he's as dirty as you, he won't be living around here. This area is far too superior for the likes of you. Now move on. We don't want your kind around here."

Jack frowned and sighed deeply. *He's not a cheerful man. Perhaps I should have stayed with Mrs Kipling and played games.* He wished he was still them as he felt his eyes begin to water. It was getting late, and he resigned himself to a night on the streets. Now he just needed a suitable place to sleep. Sheltered if possible.

As he walked through the village, looking in the shop windows that still their lights on, he wished he had a rich family that would buy him beautiful Christmas gifts. Everything looked so pretty when it got dark. Inside and outside a few shops and houses, candles and gas lights reflected an orange glow, with falling snow as a backdrop.

He found another ginnel between two shops. He warmed his hands up using his breath, slid with his back against the stone wall onto the cold, hard ground, and ate an apple out of his bindle. It had been six hours since he had eaten anything, and his belly kept making loud noises, reminding him he needed food. He picked off every piece of juicy flesh from the core, then tossed it away. As he closed his eyes, the only thing that took his mind off the cold seeping into his bones, was the thought of his mother and the Christmas carol she used to sing to him as he fell asleep.

'Silent night, holy night!
All is calm, all is bright.
Round yon Virgin, Mother and Child.
Holy infant, so tender and mild,
Sleep in heavenly peace,
Sleep in heavenly peace.'

Jack didn't realise he was singing out loud until someone threw a penny at him. He looked up and saw a young girl with her father. He noticed she was wearing a purple velvet coat and bonnet, and knee-length white socks. All of her clean clothes looked brand new.

The young girl walked on with her father, hand in hand, she looked back towards Jack and glanced at him. Clara did not know who the young boy was, but she couldn't stop staring at him. She tilted her head and squinted her eyes.

"Father, why is he wearing dirty clothes? Do you think he will be okay?"

"So many questions, Clara. You are curious, aren't you? He looks homeless, but a kind woman might have taken him in. Mrs Braithwaite told me yesterday."

Jack looked up at the father and daughter whilst crossing his fingers behind his back.

George let go of his daughter's hand, reached inside his pocket, and felt for a penny to throw at the boy.

"Thanks, mister, I'll treasure it." Jack kissed the coin and put it in his coat pocket. He wasn't willing to put that in his bindle at the risk of it being stolen whilst he was sleeping. He gazed ahead and wondered what it would be like for his father to hold his hand with warmth and love. Instead, he brought himself back to where he was, cold and shivering in the ginnel with a crown, two pennies, and some fruit and sandwiches to his name.

I must find my Uncle Cecil tomorrow. Then, without noticing, his eyes closed.

As darkness fell, Mrs Blackshaw from the apothecary on the other side of the street watched him. *Poor little soul, nowhere to go. But I can't have him sleeping at my house, there is no room.*

She opened the shop door and walked over to the young boy. Mrs Blackshaw smiled at the young lad, then crouched down and shook his arm. Jack opened his eyes and she could see his bottom lip was trembling.

"You can't stay here, where are your ma and pa?"

"I'm sorry, missus. I'll move on."

"I don't mean for you to move on, I'm just wondering where your parents are. They wouldn't let you sleep out in the cold like this, surely? You'll catch a terrible cold or worse. Hypothermia if you stay here all night. I can't have you at home because I don't have room. But if you promise not to touch anything, you can sleep in the shop."

Jack followed the woman's eyes towards the apothecary and smiled. "I have to go and sing first, miss. I'm sure I can collect a few more pennies."

"Okay, well just come to the shop when you're ready, but don't be late. I'll be closing up in an hour, so if you come back any later, that will be your chance of shelter for the night gone."

"I won't be long, promise."

"When you come back, I have some old sheets you can use. It won't be comfortable, but it will be a little warmer than outside. Please, don't be stealing anything or you'll get me in trouble," she said, eyeing him suspiciously.

"I give you my word."

Mrs Blackshaw sighed, then looked up to the sky and crossed her fingers before returning to the apothecary to serve the last customers of the day.

That night, after dinner, George asked for tea and coffee to be served in the drawing room. Margaret brought up a tray of hot drinks and placed them on the mahogany table. George walked over to the coffee pot and poured his wife a cup of the steaming hot, brown liquid. Despite feeling guilty, he concluded he knew there was no other choice.

He took the arsenic out of his pocket whilst Esther had her back to him and dropped a little in her hot coffee. *This will quieten her down.* He stirred it with milk, then put the cup and saucer on the table next to her. "There you are, my love. Drink up whilst it's hot. It's a cold evening and the snow is getting heavier. It's going to freeze tonight, the ground is already rock hard. This will warm you up." George looked at Esther and took a deep, pained breath.

Esther ignored her husband, picked up the cup, and took a sip.

Meanwhile, outside, a young boy in tattered clothes and holding a gimbal, sang his heart out.

Jack had tirelessly searched for Cecil all day, only to find bad news at every shop. "Sorry, son, no one named Cecil here, try next door."

After another day without finding his uncle, the runaway decided he would sing carols from door to door. Maybe some charitable strangers would take pity on him and reward his voice. It was Christmas, after all.

Clara leapt up from the chair and hurried over to the window. "Look, father, it's that young boy again."

"So it is, Clara. Your mother is asleep, so let's go and hear him sing and give him a penny."

George and Clara went to the front door and opened it. A rush of cold air hit them both and Clara shivered a little. She reached for her father's hand and felt the warm clasp of his fingers.

With the snow falling on the ground, and the glow of warm orange gas lights, the feeling of love and festivity was upon Clara and George. The young girl looked up at her father and pouted a little.

"Don't worry, Clara, I'm sure he has somewhere to sleep tonight."

George smiled at Jack, then walked down the imposing stone steps leading to the drive, and passed him a penny.

"There you are, son. Don't spend it all at once."

Jack let out a gasp. "Thank you, sir."

"You're very welcome. I hope you have somewhere to stay tonight."

Jack hesitated. "Erm—yes, sir, I do." He bit his bottom lip.

"Are you sure? You don't sound convinced?"

"I'll be okay, I have some friends back in the village." Jack started rubbing his hands back and forth and blew into his palms.

George looked around at his daughter, she smiled and licked her lips with cautious hope.

"What's your name, son?"

"It's, Jack, sir." Jack frowned.

"Jack, it's freezing out here. How about a mince pie and cup of tea inside?"

Jack's eyes widened with glee. He didn't hesitate in taking up the invitation. "Yes, please."

George turned around, and Jack followed him up the steps into the entrance hall.

Clara stood with her hands in front of her and giggled slightly. "My name is Clara. I saw you on the streets earlier today. Do you not have anywhere to live?"

"Clara, let the poor lad sit down first before you ask him questions."

Jack smiled at the young girl and followed George into the drawing room. "Sit down, Jack. I'll have some tea and mince pies brought to us."

Jack's neck and face flushed pink. "Brought to us? Do you not have a kitchen?"

George laughed and reached out to touch Jack's forearm. "We do, Jack. But Margaret, our housekeeper, will bring us what we need."

"Housekeeper?" The young boy opened his mouth wide, then snapped it shut quickly to avoid any further embarrassment.

"Where are you from, Jack?"

"I used to live in Brampton Town, but my ma sent me away to find my Uncle Cecil. I haven't found him yet though. Maybe tomorrow."

"Why did she do that?"

"Clara, give the poor lad a chance to drink his tea."

"So my pa wouldn't beat me up."

George thought he could see Jack's eyes watering. He then looked at his daughter and noticed her frowning.

Clara left her chair and sat next to the boy she barely knew. She slowly reached out for his hand and held it, sharing a connection through their eyes and smiles.

"It's okay, Jack, I know what that's like."

Jack looked at George and raised his eyebrows.

"Oh no, not papa. My—"

"Clara, that's enough. Jack doesn't need to know all our business. We don't even know him."

"Sorry, papa."

"Tell me, Jack," George changed the subject, "do you have somewhere to stay, or are you pretending?"

"No—no—, sir. I have somewhere to stay. I must go though, it's getting late."

George's eyes narrowed. "Is that right? You wouldn't lie because you're embarrassed, would you?"

Jack made his hand into a fist, brought it up to his mouth, and coughed. "No—no, sir, I wouldn't."

"Very well, I hope the mince pies and tea warms you up." George stood up, walked over to the table and took three mince pies. He then wrapped them in a serviette and handed them to the carol singer. "Here, take these."

"Thanks, Mister," he said, stuffing them into his pocket. "Maybe I will see you soon."

"I hope so," Clara said, sucking in her bottom lip.

Why didn't I tell the truth? Perhaps they would have let me stay. Jack reluctantly prepared for another night on his own. But with a warm, full belly of mince pies and tea, the evening brought a smile to his face. He skipped on the snowy cobbles back to Mrs Braithwaite's shop where he settled down and allowed his eyes to close.

When Jack had left, father and daughter walked to the drawing room.

"Mama is fast asleep. She must be tired."

"Yes, she is, let's not disturb her. We will see her in the morning." George covered his wife with a blanket, leaned over her, resting his hands on the arms of the chair, then kissed her goodnight on the forehead.

Chapter 11

J ack woke up cold and hungry. The shop floor had been uncomfortable. It was better than the streets, but not warm enough to stop his shivering. When he opened his eyes, it brought him back to reality. Cold, hungry, and homeless until he found his dear Uncle Cecil. He wondered how his mother was as he left her in such a state. He certainly did not trust his father to treat her kindly.

Jack heard the key in the door. He threw the sheets off him and lifted himself up onto his elbows.

"Good morning, young man. How did you sleep last night? If you were on the streets, you would have suffered worse in the cold. It's a good job I saw you. Sorry I couldn't do any more for you, but hopefully I helped a bit. I couldn't leave you sleeping outside all night, you would have got frostbite.

"I slept well thank you, it was kind of you to let me stay."

Mrs Blackshaw dismissed his thanks with a wave of her hand. "What are you going to do today? It won't be another night on the streets will it?" Mrs Blackshaw busied herself straightening bottles on the shelves ready for opening time.

"I am looking for my Uncle Cecil. My ma has sent me to find him and live with him until she catches me up."

"Why would you want to do that? Why did your mother send you on this journey alone? There must be something wrong at home for your ma to do that."

"Not much. My ma told me to run away and not return. I don't think she likes my pa very much."

Mrs Blackshaw stopped what she was doing as she felt a thud in her chest. She could only imagine what had been happening at the young lad's house. She had nothing but sympathy for the young boy standing in front of her. "Do you know where your Uncle Cecil works?"

"Ma told me he worked in the City of London, miss. Something about making suits and costumes. I must go and find him."

Mrs Blackshaw looked at Jack. She clasped her hands together and gave him a pained look. "Do you know his surname? I might be able to help."

"No," Jack shook his head. "I don't."

She sighed and tilted her head to one side. "I'm sorry, son, but I can't help you. I have never heard of anybody called Cecil, and I know of almost everyone around her."

"If you hear of him, please tell him Jack is looking for him."

"Yes, of course I will. But where will I find you?"

"You will find me around, I hope." The young hopeless boy turned around and walked out of the shop. With a tear in her eye, Mrs Blackshaw knew she wouldn't see the young boy again if the cold got to him. *Dear oh dear. I hope that the poor lad finds him soon.* She shook her head, picked the sheets up off the floor and folded them, then turned the *closed* sign around to *open*.

Jack felt disheartened. He couldn't remember which shop his Uncle Cecil worked in. He didn't know if he was in the right place. He was sure that his mother had said the City of London. But this looked more like a village. He panicked, fearing he may never find his uncle and become homeless forever.

As Jack continued to walk up the street, he came across a lady selling loaves of bread. He thought about taking one from the stall and running off with it when she wasn't looking. But his mother had always brought him up with good manners.

"Young boy! Don't you be thinking of pinching my bread! It's half a penny per loaf if you want one."

Jack was so hungry. He took a penny out of his pocket and gave it to the lady. She passed him the freshly baked crusty, white loaf. Jack lifted the baked dough up to his face and inhaled through his nose. The warming, comforting scent brought a smile to face, and he closed his eyes.

"You look as if you're homeless, young man. Where do you live?"

"I live miles away from here. My mother has told me to run away and find my Uncle Cecil. Have you heard of him?"

"Uncle Cecil? Haha, no, certainly not by that name," she said, followed by a big hearty laugh. "I don't know everybody in this village. What does he look like?"

"I don't know. I have never met him. I was just asked to find him.

"And where's your mother now?" Mrs Wilkinson said as she served another customer. "It's dangerous to be outside on your own in this weather."

Jack was tired of repeating the same story. He decided it would be wise to tell it one last time. He repeated to the bread lady what he had told Mrs Blackshaw.

"You'll catch the death of a cold whilst looking for him. Particularly if you have nowhere to stay."

Jack gazed to the ground. The temporary feeling of heartiness from sniffing the bread disappeared.

"Hey, William, come over here for a minute, will you?" The bread lady shouted over to a man walking down the street in his three-quarter length black coat and cream jodhpurs.

"Good morning, Mrs Wilkinson, how are you?"

"This young boy is looking for his Uncle Cecil and has nowhere to stay. Do you have anywhere he can sleep in exchange for some stable work?" Mrs Wilkinson said, ignoring William's pleasantries.

"I'm sure I can find him something. What is your name?" William towered over Jack and loomed over him, waiting for an answer.

"I didn't mean for the lady to ask for work for me, I'm just trying to find my uncle. Not that I'm ungrateful or anything. It's just that I have to find him."

"I'm sure you will need shelter before continuing on your journey. What is your name? You didn't say."

"It's Jack, sir."

"Come back with me to the stables and I will give you hot food and somewhere warm to stay for a couple of nights."

Remembering what it was like staying with the Kipling family, he nodded at the tall gentleman in front of him.

"Thank you."

"Come with me."

"Thank you, William." Mrs Wilkinson said, giving him a voluptuous smile and crossing her fingers behind her back. She swung her hips from side to side and watched him walk away, hoping for some personal attention from the dashing estate manager.

William looked back at Mrs Wilkinson and gave her a wave. "Have a good day, Mrs Wilkinson."

Jack wasn't sure what to expect but it was nothing as grand as what stood in front of him. He looked up at the Walker's house which was three stories high, eight windows wide, and a double door framed by a stone archway. William walked past the house towards the stables.

"Thanks for the soup, mister," Jack said, slurping the hot, gloopy wet liquid.

Dear, oh dear, the young lad must be starving to eat it as quick as that. I'm surprised it's not burned his tongue. Ada, the housekeeper, stared at the boy, shook her head and shuffled her way back to the kitchen.

When Jack had finished eating the soup, he wiped the remnants off his chin with his sleeve.

William frowned. He couldn't seem to stop staring at the young boy with no manners.

"Delicious," Jack said, emptying the bowl. He put the empty bowl down on the bale of hay next to him. "What do you want me to do, mister? I can put my hand to anything."

William took a few seconds to stop staring in disbelief. "Let's start and see how good you are at mucking out."

Jack stood up hastily and picked up a pitch fork.

"Are you a stable hand, Mister?" Jack asked whilst shoveling the mix of hay and manure to one side of the stable.

"Not quite."

"What do you do here then?"

William stopped for a moment in thought. He raised his eyebrows and let out a breath. "I suppose you could say I'm the Walker family's confidante. I help them with all their affairs and manage the house and grounds for them. I've known them for so long, they would trust me with their lives."

"It must be nice having a family like that," Jack said solemnly.

William watched the young lad and wondered what he had been through to say such a thing. He noticed he worked quickly and methodically, bringing a smile to his face. *I love hard workers, this one may be worth keeping.* "Jack, I think you'll be fine here for a few days. You seem to know what you are doing. Have you done this before?"

Jack nodded. "I helped out Farmer Carter down the road. He always had stuff for me to do. I liked looking after the horses."

"Looks like he taught you well. Keep working like this and I'll bring you hot food from the kitchen morning, noon, and night. At least you won't starve for a while. Do you think you will find your Uncle Cecil?"

"I really hope so." Jack gazed towards the ground. "I would like to see my ma, but if I go back home, I might make it worse for her."

"Why would you do that?"

Jack shrugged his shoulders. "I just would."

William sympathised with Jack but was at a loss for words. "Stay here as long as you need, you'll be fine." He patted the young boy's shoulder before walking off.

"Thank you, sir."

"Don't keep calling me that, William will be fine. Try to get some rest," William said, looking back at the boy.

The young boy lay on his back, gazing at the stable entrance. The open doors revealed a starry sky against the dark backdrop. Instead of falling asleep, he stood up, then walked outside. Jack noticed the lights on through the windows of the main house. He started to sing

Christmas carols to himself, thinking he was being quiet. But his voice echoed clearly in the silence of the night.

"Jack! I thought you were sleeping in the stables." William heard Jack's voice singing sweetly. He opened the front door to see Jack standing on the doorstep.

Jack stopped. "I was, but decided to sing a little. It helps remind me of my ma."

Where did you learn to sing with such a great voice?"

"I didn't, I just listened to ma as she sang me to sleep every night. Someone threw a penny at me for singing Silent Night the night before last. I still have it, look!" Jack reached deep into his pocket and brought out the shiny penny for his new friend to see.

That's a good way to make money. I expect it was one of the house owners from around here that gave you that. They can be very generous. Have you thought about singing some more?"

"No, I haven't."

"Maybe you should. People are still in a festive mood. Take a walk up the road and see how it goes. Then come back here and settle down for the night. It can get nice and warm in the stables with all the hay. I'll bring you some extra blankets and an oil lamp from the house, too."

The conversation with William had raised the young boy's spirits, and he walked hastily to the next house to spread some post-Christmas cheer.

Chapter 12

"Good morning, young man," William said as he saw Jack buried between hay and blankets. "Did you sleep well last night?"

"I did. But before that, I did what you said and sang. Do you remember I told you about the gentleman who had thrown a penny at me? He lives next door!" Jack said excitedly.

"Oh yes, Mr Cavendish? He lives there with his wife and daughter, Clara."

"I saw her too, she came to the door with him."

"Clara comes to the stables most days. I chat to her because I think she is lonely and her mama gives her a hard time."

"Oh, that's a shame." Just as the words had left his mouth, the young boy saw Clara approach the stables.

"Speaking of Clara, here she is. The little lady herself. Good morning, Clara, how are you today?"

"I'm fine, thank you. What's your name?" She said, smiling.

"I'm Jack. I'm staying here for a while until I find my uncle."

"You're the boy from the streets who sings Christmas carols, my father gave you some money last night, and the other day too."

"Yes, he did, and I'm very grateful."

"Here you go, Jack, sit and eat this before you start work. It's hot porridge."

Jack took the steaming hot bowl of porridge and warm cup of tea from William. He smiled with delight and blew on each mouthful before the food touched his tongue. Jack could not believe his luck. He didn't understand why people were being so kind to him. Years of his dad's cruelty made kindness unfamiliar to him.

"Thank you." Jack's eating habits left a lot to be desired. Slurping loudly on the hot porridge and tea, Clara and William watched with curiosity.

"When did you last see your uncle, Jack?"

"I've never met him, I don't think so anyway."

"Why are you asking about his uncle?"

"Because Jack is searching for him. Isn't that right, Jack?"

Jack hesitated. He was starting to feel embarrassed about the situation. Mentioning his uncle meant bringing up his pa, something he didn't want to do anymore.

"Why are you looking for him?" Clara stood in front of Jack waiting for an answer. She noticed his hesitation.

Jack looked up at Clara, then carried on eating his breakfast.

"It's okay, you can tell us. We won't say a word." Clara smiled empathetically at her new friend, noticing his shyness.

"He just wasn't nice to us, and I always felt scared around him. Sometimes I would feel his belt on the back of my legs." He stood up, lifted his trousers up and revealed his scars.

Clara gasped. "That's horrible, Jack, and I know what it feels like." She got closer to him and pointed out the bruises on her face and arms.

Jack felt relief knowing he wasn't alone in his suffering but was unsure what to say to her so he shrugged his shoulders a little and looked glum.

William changed the subject quickly. If it's one thing he didn't like to hear, was children being beaten by their parents. "I am sure you will find him soon. In the meantime, we are happy to have you here for work and rest. And I'm sure Clara will keep you company too, won't you, Clara?"

Clara smiled at Jack in acknowledgement of William's request, and he smiled back.

"Right, Jack, now you've eaten that porridge I need to introduce you to the rest of the house. Come with me. You are coming too, Clara."

Jack slowly reached for Clara's hand and they both followed William into the house. He smiled to himself at the thought of his luck changing.

"Do you like singing, Jack?" Clara said as they followed William. Perhaps you'll be a singer on the stage when you grow up."

"I couldn't imagine singing in front of lots of people. I'm too shy and not lucky enough."

Clara looked at Jack and raised her eyebrows. "You have to have Christmas wishes, have you heard of them before? Every Christmas you make a wish and then hope it will come true. A bit like a miracle."

"What do you dream about?"

"My mama loving me, marrying someone so I can wear a beautiful dress, and having lots of children."

"A nice family is all I want."

"Hello you three," Ada said as she saw William and the two young children enter the scullery. Her smile extended from ear to ear below her rosy-pink cheeks.

"Ada, you met Jack yesterday, he's going to be with us for a while. You know Clara."

"Morning Clara."

"Good morning, are you making scones today? I can smell them in the oven already."

"I am, and if you play nice, I will give you one each later."

"Hello, William!"

Jack and Clara looked around to see where the unfamiliar voice came from.

"Good morning, Isabella. Jack, Clara, this is Isabella. The Walker's granddaughter, who has come here to learn some manners," William said, rolling his eyes.

"No, I haven't," she said, knocking a sieve off the kitchen shelf on purpose to provoke a reaction.

Jack giggled. Clara just stared at her.

"You'll get shouted at for that, it's not nice."

"You'll get shouted at for that, it's not nice." Isabella mocked in a high-pitched voice.

"Right. Isabella, come on, be off with you, I have cooking to do," Ada went back to her baking whilst Jack and Clara followed William out of the house.

"She's not very nice, William."

"She's okay really, she just needs to learn some etiquette. Her parents have sent her here as she is too much to handle whilst her mother is poorly."

"What's wrong with her mother?"

"She has Diptheria," he said, dismissively. Time to go back to the stables, Jack. Clara, are you staying or are you going? If you are staying, I have plenty of mucking out you can do!"

"Ugh, no thanks. I will see you later."

Jack smiled as he watched Clara leave. *I'm starting to like it here*, he thought to himself as he grabbed a shovel and started to clean the stables.

Chapter 13

"Esther, wake up, Esther." George shook his wife's shoulder. Beads of sweat dripped from her brow. George pushed her eyelids open with his thumb and saw nothing but darkness. Please don't die, Esther, that wasn't my intention. His heart raced and thumped in his chest. He didn't know what to do.

"Please help me, George, I need—I need some water."

George looked at his wife. He let her hands flop into her lap and ran to the kitchen. He slid on the tiled floor nearly losing his footing. Turning the copper tap, he reached for a glass and filled it. He then rushed back to the drawing room where his wife sat, helplessly kneeling down in front of her and putting the glass to her lips.

Esther took a few sips, then rested her head against the chair and closed her eyes, feeling exhausted.

I can't believe I caused this, she needs a doctor quickly.

George called for the doctor and paced up and down the entrance hall biting his fingernails waiting for him to arrive. He looked at his watch as time seemed to move slowly. *What have I done, what have I done? I just wanted to quieten her down and stop her shouting at Clara.*

Three loud bangs hit the front door. George rushed towards the door and opened it. "Thank you for coming, doctor."

"You're lucky. I've been busy all day treating patients with diphtheria and have just finished doing my rounds. Now, where is she?" He followed George into the drawing room.

"She's been asleep ever since I called you. She took only a few sips of water. Can you do something?"

Doctor Harrison placed one hand on Esther's forehead and felt for a pulse in her wrist with the other. He closed his eyes and tilted his head back to the ceiling, silently counting. "Her pulse is weak. This is very worrying. Do you know how she caught this dreadful illness?"

"Illness?" George's eyebrows furrowed together. "Erm—erm, no I don't." He brought his fingers to his parted lips. Doctor, what disease do you think it is?"

"Her swollen throat and fever show that she most definitely has diphtheria. How long has she been like this?"

George cleared his throat. "I'm—I'm not sure, doctor. I know she stayed down here all night, and I noticed she was delirious when I tried to wake her earlier. She couldn't take much water though and was sweating profusely." George looked at the doctor and prayed in his mind.

"It might be from the water supply. There is plenty of diphtheria going around. I suggest you boil all your water for the next week, if only in an attempt to stop you and your daughter catching this dreadful illness too."

"What should we do in the meantime, doctor?""

"She could try inhaling iodine to see if that helps. Unfortunately, there's not much else we can do. Allow her to rest and keep her hydrated as much as possible."

"And you're sure it's diphtheria?" George crossed his arms and bit his lip. He glanced over towards Esther.

"I'm almost certain. Why do you ask?"

"Oh, no reason. I suppose I just want to know so I can try to stop Clara catching it, too."

"Like I say, boil your water." The doctor looked at George, then patted his back. "I am sorry George."

"Thank you—I will keep an eye on her. Can I call you again if she worsens?"

"By all means, yes. If she needs anything else, I'll come over."

George nodded in acknowledgement. "Thank you for coming. I shall see you out."

Doctor Harrison turned towards George before leaving. "I'm sorry, George, so sorry." He touched George's elbow before turning around and walking down the steps with his black bag.

George clicked the door shut and walked back to the drawing room. He covered Esther with a blanket and held her hand. He sighed, feeling guilty for what he had done, but relieved it seemed it wasn't the arsenic after all.

At least he and Clara had some respite from the familiar shouting and beatings.

Chapter 14

C lara saw her father sitting in the drawing room. "Is mama awake yet?"

George looked up, the rims around his eyes were red and he stifled a yawn. He reached out his arms to his daughter.

Clara ran over to George and sat on his knee. She put her arms around his neck and leaned into his shoulder.

"No, she isn't Clara. She is poorly. I need to talk to you for a minute. Your mother is very sick and I—"

Clara interjected. "Will she wake up?"

"Oh, Clara." Tears started to fall down his cheeks.

"Don't cry, papa, you always have me."

"I know, and I love you so much. We will have to get through this together. I'm not sure she will wake up, but we'll see."

Clara looked at her father emotionlessly and shrugged her shoulders. "She was never very nice to me anyway."

"I know that, but it doesn't mean we wish her harm, does it?"

Clara shook her head.

"We just need to be here for her now."

Later that day, Clara and George ate their dinner in silence. As they finished their evening meal, George went back up the stairs to check on his wife having carried her to bed after the doctor had been. He opened the door to the darkened bedroom and heard her breathing, laboured and shallow. He walked over to his wife and noticed her pillow was wet from her sweat.

George took hold of his wife's hand and kissed it. "I'm here for you, my love. I'm so sorry you are sick." He rested his head on her hand and felt her fingers twitch. He looked up and saw she tried to speak.

"Yes, Esther? What is it, tell me?"

"Clara, please tell her—" Esther said, squeezing George's hand whilst contorting a little with the pain. "Please tell her—"

"Please tell her what, Esther, I don't understand?"

"Please tell her—" Esther took her last gasp of breath.

"No, no. Please, Esther." He showered her hand in kisses and stroked her forehead. "I'm sorry I've not been a better husband, I'm sorry. I should have helped you more, I love you." He wiped his tears away with his hand then rested his forehead on her torso. "I love you, Esther."

Sorrowfully, he clasped his hands together and said a prayer.

'Our Father who art in heaven,
hallowed be thy name;
thy kingdom come,

thy will be done;
on earth as it is in heaven.
Give us this day our daily bread.
And forgive us our trespasses
as we forgive those who trespass against us.
And lead us not into temptation;
but deliver us from evil.
For thine is the kingdom,
the power,
and the glory, for ever and ever.
Amen.'

After waiting a few minutes, he stood up and walked out of her bedroom, slowly closing the door as if not to disturb her from her permanent state of sleeping. Now he had to tell his daughter what had happened. He crossed the carpeted landing and knocked on Clara's bedroom door.

Clara looked at George.

"I know, papa."

He rushed over to her and sat on the side of her bed. "How do you know?"

Clara shrugged her shoulders. "Don't cry, papa, she's asleep now. Not that I'll miss her very much."

"I'm sorry, Clara."

"I know mama was very poorly, but she won't be in pain now, will she? And Henry will have his mama with him in heaven."

George looked at his daughter and the fading bruises under her eyes. He never wanted Esther to die, he just wanted the shouting to stop. The love he had for his daughter was unrequited and, he would do anything to save her from pain.

"Yes, he will." George wrapped his daughter in his arms and kissed her on the top of her head. "It's just us now."

Clara nodded a little then stood up and walked over to the window. She stared out of the window and watched the heavy snowflakes falling outside as young children threw the soft snow into the air and laughed. "I'll never be like my mama, never. When I have a family, I will love them properly."

George noticed a fierceness and determination in his daughter's voice. "I know you will, Clara. I know you will." He looked at his daughter and wondered what the future held for her.

Chapter 15

"Hello," Jack said. "I didn't catch your name before." He looked at the beautiful girl with big brown eyes standing in front of him.

"It's Isabella, silly. I'm here to stay with my grandparents and Uncle William for a couple of months. My mother is sick and cannot look after me. I feel like I've been here forever. What are you doing here?"

"I help in the stables, I'm also trying to find my uncle."

"Where is he?"

"I don't know."

Isabella wrinkled her nose and stuck out her tongue. She turned and began walking away.

Jack grimaced.

"Where are your mama and papa? Do you not have any?"

The question brought a stab to Jack's heart. "Aye, I just haven't seen them in a while."

"Why not?"

"You ask a lot of questions."

"I'm only trying to be nice, I won't bother speaking to you again." Isabella folded her arms across her chest and turned away.

"I guess I just don't want to talk much about it. My pa isn't very nice to me and ma, so I ran away to find my uncle. When I was homeless, Mrs Wilkinson, the bread seller, asked William if he had work for me."

"How long are you going to stay for?"

Jack shrugged his shoulders. "I don't know. I quite like it here, I've been learning to look after the horses."

Maybe I'll see more of you if you're staying. I don't know when I'll go home." Shall we go and play?"

"Play what?"

"Let's play hide and seek in the stables." That would be fun."

Isabella faced the stable door, covered her face with her forearms, and counted to twenty. She opened her eyes and ran off to find her new friend. She searched every stable, haystack, and the corner of the building where the tools were kept. Unable to find Jack, Isabella sighed and stamped her feet, then turned around and walked back home.

"Boo!"

Isabella held a hand to her chest and jumped. "Stupid, you gave me a fright," she said, giving her new friend a shove in his chest which almost sent Jack backwards.

Isabella relaxed a little and gave Jack a mischievous smile.

"Just kidding, you might have scared me a bit, but it was fun."

The two children burst into laughter and started rolling around on top of the hay bales.

Clara walked slowly towards the Walker's house. She was desperate to speak to Jack and tell him about her mama dying. She gently bit her lip and followed the sound of laughter. Knowing her mother had died, she felt jealous hearing other children enjoy themselves.

She quietly approached and peeked around the stable door. Seeing Isabella and Jack playing together, she immediately ran back home. She slammed the front door and ran up to her bedroom. Bursting into tears, she threw herself onto her bed face down. She wasn't upset that her mother had died. She seemed happy about that, at least from the outside. Jack's new friend made Clara feel frustrated and sad.

"Are you okay, Clara?" George shouted. He raced up the stairs after his daughter when he heard the commotion. "Yes, I'm fine," she let out a little sigh.

He walked up to her bedroom door and rested the side of his face against the wood. "It's okay to be sad about your mama, you know. I'm here for you."

"No papa, I'm not sad for her. She hurt me and never loved me enough to treat me as her daughter. I never felt like she was a proper mother."

"What's wrong then, you don't seem very happy."

"Oh, it's nothing. Jack has a new friend, and I wanted to tell him what happened. I thought he would understand."

"He can have other friends, Clara."

George gently tapped on her door, then walked into his daughter's bedroom and sat down on the bed beside her. He stroked her hair behind her ears and smiled.

"What will happen now, is mama having a funeral?" she asked, changing the subject.

"The undertaker has been to take her away, and will arrange for her to be buried as soon as possible."

"Do you know why she died so quickly?"

"Not really, Clara. Only that she had caught a dreadful illness and that she was in pain towards the end. Your mother just wasn't strong enough to live any longer. Your baby brother will be with her in heaven now though.

Clara looked at her dad. "Well, I hope she is nice to him. I'd rather not go to the funeral. I'm happy now she's gone."

George knew he couldn't persuade his daughter to go to the funeral. He wasn't fooled by her dismissive attitude and lack of grief either. He knew how death affected you as a young child, he'd lived through enough of it himself.

He left his daughter in her room and went downstairs. He was about to pour himself a whisky when the doorbell rang out.

"Hello, Jack, how are you?"

"I'm very well thanks, sir. I've come to sing a final Christmas carol." Jack stood on his tiptoes and moved his head to the side to look behind George.

"Are you okay, Jack? Are you looking for something?"

"I wondered if Clara was in? I thought she might like to listen."

"Clara. Clara?" George stood at the bottom of the stairs waiting for his daughter to come down, but there was no sign of her. "I'm sorry, Jack, she isn't coming down tonight, maybe she's in bed already."

Mid song, the young boy's eyes were drawn up towards Clara's bedroom window. Looking solemn, she looked down at Jack. No welcoming smiles were seen from her this time. Jack wondered what was wrong with her as he finished his Christmas carol.

"Thank you, Jack, that was wonderful."

Jack didn't say anything. Jack's head hung low as he walked back to the stables. He didn't turn around once to look at Clara again. Her ignorance was too hurtful for him to bear.

Chapter 16

EIGHT YEARS LATER

"Are you joining us for our Christmas family dinner, Jack?"

"I would love to, William."

"Do you think Clara and George would like to join us?"

"I will ask them. Thank you for asking me to invite them."

"Nonsense. We have known them for years. It's hard for them both at this time of year. Will Clara be singing with you on Christmas day in the village square?"

"I hope so. I keep thinking that one year she may finally grieve for losing her mother. But—"

"But what, Jack?"

"I don't know. It's like she has completely blanked her out of her memory."

"Her mother didn't treat her well. There was much speculation about what George and Clara went through after Esther's death. It's fortunate the doctor said she died of diphtheria."

"Why's that?"

"Because some of us might have suspected George's involvement in her death."

"Esther's behaviour couldn't have been that bad for George to kill her, surely?"

"You only had to look at Clara some days to see she had been beaten black and blue. It was almost like Esther blamed her daughter for Henry's death.

A wave of sadness washed over Jack. "I should have been there for her more often. I didn't know her very well. But I always felt we had a close bond."

"You can't turn back time, Jack. You were only a young boy yourself at the time."

Jack momentarily closed his eyes and his heart felt heavy. He briefly shook his head and then regained his senses.

"You're not in love with her are you, Jack?"

"In love with Clara?" He cleared his throat and laughed a little. "Oh no, not at all. She is just a friend. "I'm marrying Isabella, and from what I hear, her parents are delighted."

William's eyes squinted for a split second. Enough for him to doubt what Jack was telling him. "We should sit down, dinner will be ready soon."

Jack followed William into the dining room. "Isabella, you look beautiful." The deep green dress that Isabella was wearing had caught

Jack's eye as she walked down the stairs. He took hold of her hand and led her to the chair next to him.

"Jack, I'm going to write and send all the Christmas cards. I think it's a good idea to send joint ones now, don't you?"

"Yes, of course, that's a lovely idea." Jack forced a smile, but still felt a heaviness in his chest.

"Are you out singing tonight, Jack? I know everyone is looking forward to it. Christmas carols always help us get into the festive spirit.

"I am, yes, Charlotte. Are you going to come and watch?"

"I'm not sure. I'll be there if Jessica can look after Sophia."

Jack looked at Charlotte, William's wife, and couldn't help but notice how in love they were. The affectionate expressions and hand holding under the table was what he should have been doing with Isabella. But someone else was always on his mind, stopping him from giving Isabella the love and affection she deserved.

"She is growing up fast, soon she will be crawling I expect." Jack cleared his throat a little as his eyes started to water.

"Are you okay, Jack? You seem upset." Charlotte stood up from the table and lifted her daughter out of the highchair.

"Erm—no, no, I'm fine."

"You don't seem it, Jack. Can I get you something?"

"Honestly, I'm quite alright. I was thinking of Clara without her mother this year and what she went through as a child. I can't ever imagine anyone treating their daughter like that. Seeing you both love Sophia like you do, makes me feel sorry for Clara."

Isabella rolled her eyes and slammed her knife and fork down onto her plate.

"Is anything wrong?" Jack looked sideways at his fiancé.

"No."

"Your body language tells me differently, Isabella. You're not jealous of me talking about Clara, are you?"

"I think I am a little. She seems to be your favourite person."

"Isabella, don't be like that."

"Well, you're not exactly denying it, are you?" Isabella looked at Jack with wide, stone-cold eyes."

"I'm not sure there is anything to deny. Clara and I have always been friends, as you know."

"And don't I know it."

Sophia started to cry, and William changed the subject. "Do you think you will ever find your uncle next year, Jack? I know the trail went cold, but it doesn't mean you should stop looking."

"I've nearly stopped searching for him after all this time. I still don't know how my mother is despite me writing to her."

"Why don't you go and visit her with Isabella? I'm sure it would please her to see you. Won't she be thrilled when she finds out you're getting married?"

"I'm not so sure it's a good idea. I will think about it," he said dismissively.

"I wonder if you would feel differently if you had a different fiancé?"

"Isabella, let's not start this again, you're being ridiculous."

"Am I?

Jack took a deep breath in and finished his dinner. Nobody spoke for the rest of the meal.

"I'm going out now, otherwise I will be late. I will see you all soon. If you are coming to watch us sing, we will see you shortly." Jack threw his serviette down at the side of his dinner plate and stormed out of the room.

Isabella tucked a loose piece of hair behind her ear and did all that she could to stop her tears from flowing in front of William and Charlotte.

Chapter 17

As Jack walked down the cobbled street, slippy and white from the compacted snow, he couldn't help but feel excited about seeing Clara. Singing with her was the main reason he loved this time of year.

He swallowed down his emotion from the evening before knocking on Clara's front door. He hesitated and nervously tapped his foot. He had felt bothered and annoyed at being questioned by Isabella about Clara. He knew they were only friends since she had given him a penny years ago. Yet he yearned for more.

"Are you okay, Jack, you look shocked."

"I—erm—oh, I didn't even knock."

"I know. I saw you from the window. I thought, any moment now he will knock on the door. But you just stood there as if you were contemplating calling for me. Are you sure there is nothing wrong?"

Jack was mesmerised. He tried hard not to let his eyes wander over Clara's slender frame and the beautiful gown she was wearing. "I'm okay, I just had a minor disagreement with Isabella, but it will be fine. We can talk later."

Clara squinted. "I guess we should go then, or we'll be late."

Jack nodded once and led the way. "Can I just say—"

"Yes, Jack?"

"You look beautiful tonight."

Clara felt a flutter in her chest. "Thank you." She looked down at her deep burgundy satin dress and turned from side to side with a smile on her face. "You like it then? My new dress? It's an early Christmas gift from my father."

"The colour really suits you."

"Thank you, Jack, and you look very handsome."

Jack put his hand on his hip and held out his arm for Clara to link on to. Anybody who didn't know them, would have thought they were courting.

"Jack, I have something to tell you." Clara slowed down a little. "Erm—" she scratched the back of her neck and drew in a deep breath.

"What is it? Are you getting married?" His stomach flipped hoping she wasn't going to give him the news he dreaded. He didn't know how he would cope seeing her marry someone else. Jack knew his feelings were wrong. He was engaged to be married to Isabella, and he felt he was betraying her just by thinking of Clara.

"No, silly. I start work tomorrow."

Jack let out a sigh. "Work? What a relief."

"What do you mean by relief, Jack?"

"Erm—oh, I meant you must be relieved, but I didn't think you would have to work. I thought you would have inherited most of your mother's estate."

"I don't have to work, not really. I am eager to see more of London, meet new people, and have different experiences. It's not about the money for me. It never has been. I wouldn't have cared if she left me nothing. The wretched woman."

"You are so brave, Clara. Whatever would I do without you as a friend? Oh, I almost forgot to say, William has invited you and your father round for Christmas celebrations and dinner on Christmas Day. Would you care to join us at the Walkers?"

"Will Isabella be there?"

"Of course, she will be there, she is my fiancé."

"We would love to join you. Father is very grateful for the Walker's support after my mother's death. He wouldn't dream of turning the invitation down."

"Perfect, a joint Christmas it will be, then."

I do wish we were together though, waiting to be married. Clara couldn't help but feel jealous of Isabella. *I wish we were linking arms as husband and wife.*

"Where will you be working?"

"I will be working for a gentleman on Saville Row. He needed an assistant, and I wanted to work in London."

"London? That's at least two miles from here, how will you get there?"

"I am going to use some of my mother's inheritance. I may as well put it to good use. I have hired a groomsman to ride our horse and carriage."

"It sounds like you have it all planned out."

"I do, and I'm excited about it. I can't wait to tell you about my first day."

"That's great news, Clara. I wish you well." Jack leaned forward and pecked Clara's cheek."

"Jack? What are you thinking of? We're not—"

"I'm sorry. So sorry, I got caught up in the moment. I'm pleased for you, that's all."

Jack and Clara took their position in the village square and shared the sheet of music. Neither of them had noticed Isabella, William, and Charlotte, in the crowd.

Isabella's palm of her hand covered her mouth and her eyes welled up. She shook her head in denial and vowed silently to get her revenge.

Chapter 18

The next day, Clara walked into the shop on Saville Row. Her fingers tingled with excitement as the brass bell rang above the door.

"Good Morning, Miss Cavendish, how are you today? Clara's charm and ambition attracted Mr Dalton a couple of weeks ago. He hired her immediately.

"I am very well, thank you. I'm looking forward to my first day."

"Morning, miss." The voice appeared from behind the counter. "My name is Oliver, I help Mr Dalton three days a week"

Clara said hello, noticing Oliver's wandering eyes.

"Hello."

"Let's get you started shall we, Clara? Mr Dalton took Clara through to the back room and showed her where all the material was stored.

"This is a fantastic place, look at all these colour's and stripes." Clara said excitedly, like a child in a sweet shop. She ran her fingers over the ends of the rolls.

The back room was small and overcrowded with floor to ceiling shelves. Rolls of material, sequins, feathers, and ribbon, overflowed. But at least it looked organised.

"How much experience have you had with material and bespoke suit making?"

"Oh, not much, but I'm always willing to learn."

"How about costumes for the theatre?"

Clara winced. "Not really."

Mr Dalton noticed Clara's nervousness. "Don't worry. If it had been important, I wouldn't have hired you. When I show you the ropes, you will pick things up quickly enough. Our first appointment is with Leo Cooper, a theatre manager from the Adelphi."

"He sounds very important." No sooner had the words left her mouth, the brass bell rang again and in walked Mr Cooper.

Clara was immediately drawn to his flamboyancy. A medium height gentleman with dark hair, wore a claret colour suit. A colour Clara had not seen on a man before.

"Good morning, Mr Cooper. We have our brand new assistant starting today."

"Good morning, Miss," Mr Cooper said, lifting his black bowler hat slightly off his head in acknowledgement of the woman standing in front of him.

"Hello, sir."

"Come over here and I will take your measurements again." The tall, good looking theatre assistant followed the tailor and Clara to the back of the shop.

"What do you need today?" Mr Dalton took his tape measure out of his inside pocket.

"I think a couple of suits for the New Year, don't you? Perhaps something black and another one of a more cheerful nature. What do you think?"

"Clara, over here." Oliver called. Clara looked over to where Oliver was, he beckoned her over to the store room.

The interruption mildly irritated Clara. Leo seemed like a much more interesting character than Mr Dalton's over-keen assistant.

"We need to get these rolls of material and take them to Mr Dalton, so he can show them to Leo."

Clara held out her arms and Oliver loaded three rolls of material.

"Tell me, Clara, how will you be spending Christmas this year?"

"Oliver, that's an imposing question so soon after meeting a lady."

"I'm never one to miss a chance with a fine young woman. "

Clara blushed and gave a slight smile. She couldn't deny that Oliver was handsome and charming. "If you must know, I am having Christmas with my father and Christmas celebrations with Jack at the Walker household. I'm really looking forward to it."

"Who is Jack?"

"Don't tell me you are jealous already?"

"Just need to know who my competition is."

Clara rolled her eyes.

"Hurry you two, I want to show Clara how to measure up."

"Why won't you show me?" Oliver chimed in.

"Because, Oliver, Clara seems much more sensible and professional."

Oliver wrinkled his nose and gave Mr Dalton a stare.

"I have eyes in the side of my head, Oliver. Don't be so childish. Now, Clara, come and watch me. I'm going to measure from Leo's—" Cecil brought a fist up to his mouth and coughed a little before continuing. "Leo's groin to the bottom of his ankle, like this," he said, stretching the measuring tape up and down Leo's inside leg.

Clara's cheeks flushed pink and she turned her head away slightly from the job in hand.

"You're not shy, are you?" Leo said, looking down on the new assistant.

Clara's cheeks blushed pink, and she hesitated in measuring for a second, pulling the tape measure away.

"I'm only joking, I can see you're doing a good job."

"Thirty-one inches, Mr Dalton."

"Excellent, that's what I have as well. You're learning quickly, my dear."

"You're learning quickly, my dear," Oliver mimicked.

"Do you work with any performers, Mr Cooper?"

"I sure do. Have you heard of Nancy Franklin?"

Clara gasped. "Yes!" She stood up with a big smile on her face. "She is my favourite although I've never seen her perform. I've heard lots of good things about her though, and heard her sing on the phonograph."

"She's my best friend, I will give you tickets to see her perform one night. Consider it a welcome present to Mr Dalton's store, from me."

"Thank you, that would be wonderful. I sing with my friend Jack. Mainly at Christmas time. To be honest, he is much better than I am, I just keep him company."

"Perhaps you are a rising star," Leo said, waving his hand up in the air.

"I doubt it, Jack is the star, not me."

"Right, Leo, that will be all for today. I will let you carry on with your day. Your suits will be ready in about four weeks. Just pay me when you collect."

"A fantastic service as always, Mr Dalton, it's been a pleasure." Leo flounced out of the store.

"Why would you want to sing? Sounds a bit wishy washy to me," Oliver said.

"Not at all, it's great fun. And it brings festive cheer at this time of year. I'm singing tonight, you could always come and find me in Holly village and watch."

"What are you singing?"

"I am singing Christmas carols with Jack."

"You do a lot with Jack. Are you close to him?"

"Not like that." Clara swallowed hard. "He is one of—no, my only good friend. Besides, he has a girlfriend."

"You sound disappointed."

"Not really, I'm not sure we could get married. We have been friends forever, so it would seem a bit odd."

"In which case, would you do me the honour of having dinner with me one evening?"

"Yes, why not? I suppose it will help us get to know each other a bit better if we are going to be working together."

"Wonderful, I can't wait." Oliver said, running his tongue over his teeth.

Oliver left work later that evening with no intention of them just being friends. Meanwhile, Clara wished it was Jack she was having dinner with. Not Oliver who came across as a clumsy oaf. Clara wanted love, romance, and a real man to spend the rest of her life with. But unfortunately, he was taken.

Chapter 19

⁓⊱✦⊰⁓

"Clara, George, come in, come in. Good to see both of you."

"Thank you, William, we are looking forward to dinner," George said, shaking William's hand. "It's always a bit strange this time of year, for good reason."

"I understand, George. It must be hard on you both."

"Not in my opinion. It's been eight years since mama died, and I haven't missed her one bit." Clara shrugged the shawl off her shoulders for William to catch, then walked through to the drawing room.

William raised his eyebrows.

"Don't say anything, William. She conceals her grief behind a strong facade. I hope she realises one day what her mother went through. I don't for one moment forgive Esther's behaviour towards us both however, she was deeply affected by Henry's death. I wish she would have got help for her melancholia, I blame myself for that."

"I understand." William patted George's shoulder. "But you can't blame yourself, George, it won't do you or your daughter any good. Come on through, I'll get you a drink."

Clara stood in the corner of the drawing room. Isabella had poured her a sherry, which Clara now held in her black gloved hand. Clara didn't notice her father joining her at her side.

"Good, isn't he?"

"Huh?" Clara said.

"Jack, he's a good singer." George was equally taken with Jack's voice as his daughter was.

"Yes, he is. His voice certainly shines through above mine when we sing together." Clara noticed Isabella sat in front of her fiancé, unable to notice her facial expression. But from her relaxed shoulders and slight tilt of the head, it was obvious that she too was engrossed in Jack's performance.

George stood at the door clapping his hands in the air. "Bravo young man, bravo," George said when Jack had finished.

"Thank you, George. A merry Christmas to you and Clara. In fact, Clara, why don't you come and join me for a sing-song before we sit down for dinner?"

"I would love to, Jack." Clara walked over to the piano and brushed past Isabella with an air of confidence. Isabella did not look happy as her eyes followed George's close friend to the piano. The Erard grand piano veneered in ebony and engraved with ivory marquetry, stood in front of the window with its lid held open by its prop.

Clara and Jack looked into each other's eyes and sang *God Rest Ye Merry Gentlemen*. Unconsciously, Jack reached out for Clara's hand and drew her closer as they reached the end of the carol.

A few second's silence followed and Isabella stared open mouthed at the site in front of her. Everyone around her clapped then headed to the dining room for dinner.

Jack reached out for Isabella as they walked towards the dining room table. She brushed past him, refusing to look at her fiancé, with an expression as cold as the winter's night.

"Clara, what are your plans for the coming year? Are you going to be a lady of leisure for life? You don't want to be feeding off your mother's inheritance do you?"

"Isabella! Was it necessary to involve Clara's mother in that question?"

"It's quite alright, Jack." Clara said, smiling. Her gaze then turned to his fiancé, and she scowled. "Isabella, as you know being a lady of leisure yourself, it's not all we hoped it would be, is it? Instead of relying on a gentleman to rescue me, I work on Saville Row crafting bespoke suits for the theatre's elite".

"A job? How very uncouth of you."

"Uncouth? Far from it. You see, I have aspirations, Isabella. I want to be one of the wealthiest women in Holly village in my own name, rather than *feeding off my mother's inheritance* as you put it so eloquently. You have to start somewhere when you are so aspirational. Simply relying on others for sustenance is not acceptable. Wouldn't you agree?"

"I'm not sure about that. I am doing quite alright thank you, living here with the Walkers and almost being married to my love," Isabella said as she lifted a glass towards Jack.

"Don't exaggerate darling, we haven't quite agreed on a wedding date yet, have we?"

"It was less than three hours ago when we were discussing our future together. How would your answer have been different, Jack, if Clara wasn't here?"

"Clara is my dear friend, and I don't think we should be discussing this here." Jack exhaled and stared Isabella into submission.

"Cheers everybody!" William said, in an attempt to diffuse the current conversation. "Good tidings and good health to everyone here."

"Cheers." Everybody said as they lifted their glasses.

The Walker family and their house guests made their way to the drawing room after dinner. Isabella brushed past Clara and almost knocked the drink out of her hand.

"Be careful, look what you've made me do!"

"I'm so sorry, I didn't see you there." Isabella scowled at Clara and sat down on the sofa by the fireplace.

"Clara, I'm so sorry, let me help you clean your dress."

"It's fine, Jack, I will get Margaret to do it when I get home. Let's not allow it to ruin our evening."

Jack blotted the excess liquid from his friend's silk dress with his handkerchief. "Clara, tell me again where you are working."

"On Saville Row. A wonderful gentleman called Cecil Dalton hired me and seems thrilled with my work so far."

"That sounds—"

"Yes, Jack?"

"Wait, did you say Cecil?" And he works on Saville Row in the City of London?"

"No, surely not? Do you think he could be your uncle?"

"I don't know, it's possible. It can't be a coincidence, can it? How many other Cecil's work on Saville Row? Jack began pacing the room.

George was sitting next to his daughter and listening in on the conversation.

"Why don't you go and meet him, Jack? I'm sure Clara won't mind taking you, will you dear?" George said, glancing at his daughter.

"No, of course I wouldn't mind. It would be my absolute pleasure to help find your uncle, Jack." Clara looked at Isabella. "It's the least I can do as your *dearest* and *closest* friend."

"Oh, how exciting, Jack, I must come with you."

"No, I don't think so Isabella, it would seem too overcrowded. It's something I must do on my own."

Isabella went red in the cheeks and felt a lump in her throat. She tried everything possible to stop tears forming through sheer embarrassment by the person who she thought loved her. The young woman was beginning to question if Jack was right for her. Humiliating her and putting her second in front of the lady who appeared to enjoy prostituting herself in a job, had made Isabella feel small and unwanted.

Later in the evening, the Walkers said goodnight to their guests.

"How dare you humiliate me in front of those people with your friend!"

"Isabella. What on earth are you talking about?"

"You know damn well what I am talking about."

"We haven't agreed on a wedding date yet, so it wasn't the right time to discuss it in front of friends."

"And what about me helping you find your uncle? It's meant to be a joyous occasion. And one which I would have thought you would enjoy sharing with your fiancé."

"I didn't mean any harm, Isabella. I don't recall exactly what I said, but I didn't mean to hurt you."

"Let me recall what your words were, Jack, something like *No, I don't think so Isabella, it would seem too overcrowded.*"

"Darling, there's no need—"

"Don't you *darling* me, Jack!" Isabella threw half a glass of sherry over her fiancé's white shirt then ran off upstairs crying.

Jack had no inclination to chase after her. He sat, head in hands, yearning for the night's end and to hold Clara in his arms forever.

Chapter 20

The anticipation grew in Jack's chest. After a restless night of hot sweats and tossing and turning beneath the blanket on the sofa, he awoke feeling drowsy and nervous. As soon as his eyes opened, his stomach churned with thoughts of his parents and uncle.

He looked at the time and realised Clara would be calling for him at any minute. He ran out of the drawing room, up the stairs, and got changed. Looking in the mirror, he brushed his hair and splashed water over his face, then reached for his deep, earthy cologne and splashed a couple of dashes on his neck.

Jack looked up when he heard a knock on the door. He finished tying his laces and ran down the stairs.

"Clara, it's good to see you."

"Good, God, Jack. You look like you've hardly slept. Have you only just dressed?"

Jack raised his eyebrows and stepped outside. "God, it's cold. Hang on a moment will you?"

Clara's eyes followed him back into the entrance hall and watched him put his coat and scarf on. Jack tied the thick, deep red, woven scarf around his neck in a single knot.

"Sorry, late night."

"Thought as much. Did Isabella have anything to do with it?"

"Kind of, she wasn't best pleased when I said she couldn't come today."

Clara tried hard not to let her grin show. "Anyway, are you ready to meet him?" she said, as she stepped into the carriage.

"I am, I think. I pushed finding him out of my mind for a long time. I guess I was happy with working for the Walkers, met Isabella, and before I knew it, my life was mapped out before me."

"Oh, Jack. You sound as if you're older than your years. You are only seventeen."

"I know. When you meet someone, people assume you'll spend the rest of your life with them. Other people's expectations consume your thoughts, pushing everything else aside."

"I'm here for you, you know that don't you?"

"I do. And I just want to say, whilst I'm feeling all melancholy, that I'm so, so sorry I wasn't there for you as much as I should have been. You know. After your mother died."

Clara held Jack's hand and said, "We're good friends, that's all that matters." Clara and Jack sat next to each in the Brougham carriage, and couldn't seem to take their eyes off each other.

"Why didn't you tell me about your mother's death when you said you came to see me that day?"

Clara took her hand off his and placed it in her lap with her other. Her fingers flicked the wicks of her nails one by one.

"Clara?"

She turned around and looked at him, her eyes began to water. "I was hurting Jack. I know I said I didn't care that my mama had died. I mean, good Lord, I suffered. I needed to tell you because I was still hurting. When I heard you laughing with Isabella, I guess I got jealous. Why would you have wanted tears on your shoulder when I could see you happy instead?"

"Clara, please don't say that. You and your father threw me pennies and gave me hope when I needed it the most. Both of you were there for me as a lost boy on the streets. If it hadn't had been for you, I don't think—"

"Here we are, miss."

"Thank you, Jonathan."

Clara and Jack stepped down from the carriage and looked up at Dalton's Bespoke Tailoring.

"I don't want to surprise him or make him uncomfortable. What if he says he doesn't want to know me?"

"Jack, calm down, I'm sure he will be just fine!"

"I've waited for this moment for years, Clara. I am hoping that he is in touch with my mother. She has never once responded to me, you know. I've reached out to her countless times."

Clara reached across, took hold of Jack's hand, and squeezed it tightly. "Well, maybe she moved on and didn't want to be found. I know the feeling of longing for a better life when a loved one doesn't treat you as well as they should.

"Yes, of course, you do. I just—I just don't know what I will do if it's not him or he doesn't want to know me. Maybe ma had enough of me."

"She wouldn't have rejected you just like that. She would have had a reason for not responding. Perhaps she thought you'd be happy with your life and wanted to avoid your father knowing where you were."

"I'm not convinced. Perhaps, well, perhaps they are both dead. Dear, God, I never thought of that." His eyes started to water a little, and he squeezed Clara's hand. Perhaps losing my baby sister was too much for them both to bear."

"It sounds like we both have a history we would rather forget."

"Quite," Jack said.

"Good morning, Mr Dalton, Oliver."

"Good morning, Clara. You are looking as radiant as always. Did you have a nice Christmas?"

"I did, and you?"

"Yes, I did. It was quiet, but just fine nonetheless. Who is your friend?"

Oliver was crouched over, stacking material on the bottom shelves. He stopped what he was doing and looked around towards Clara and the gentleman stood next to her. His teeth gripped the end of his tongue.

"This is my dearest friend, Jack."

"Good morning, Jack, here for a new suit?" Or perhaps to help Clara out. Not that she needs any, her work has impressed me so far."

"Erm—well, no. I don't need a suit."

"How do you do Jack? I'm Oliver," he said as he held out his hand. "I have heard lots about you."

"Good to meet you, Oliver."

"The thing is, Mr Dalton, it is quite complicated."

"Complicated, Clara? Don't tell me you are running off and leaving your new role to get married?"

Jack blushed and Clara rolled her eyes. "Of course not. But you may have a nephew standing in front of you!"

"I'm sorry, what did you say?" The whole shop went silent.

"Mr Dalton," Jack cleared his throat. "I think—I think you might be my Uncle Cecil"

Cecil let his measuring tape and crimping scissors drop to the dark inspection table. "Come to the back room."

Jack looked at Clara and raised his eyebrows.

"You'll be fine," Clara mouthed.

"Come on, don't keep me waiting!"

Jack followed Cecil to the store room.

"One thing is for sure," Oliver said, sighing.

"What's that?"

"I've never heard Mr Dalton use that stern tone of voice before."

Clara watched Jack and Cecil leave the front of the shop, gasped a little, and wondered whether she had done the right thing.

Chapter 21

J ack's eyes darted around, seeking someone to interrupt the silence. The stillness was overbearing and made him feel uncomfortable. He pierced his lips together and wondered how Cecil Dalton was going to react to the news.

Cecil stood leaning against the inspection table with his arms folded across his chest. His eyes wandered up and down the gentleman standing in front of him.

"Are you going—are you going to say something, sir?"

Cecil stared at Jack. Not a cold, hard stare. He blinked occasionally adding some warmth to his demeanour.

Jack thought about walking away instead of facing Cecil. But he knew running now meant no return. He would be too embarrassed to face Cecil again if he didn't take the news well.

"I've been waiting for almost ten years, Jack, for this moment."

Jack's mouth fell open. He went to talk, but no sound left his mouth.

"That's right, almost ten years," Cecil said, noticing Jack's surprise.

"How did you know?"

"Your mother sent a letter. Not to this address if you're wondering. It landed at Mr Howson's apothecary ten doors down. It appears he took a chance with the address and must have assumed it would reach me somehow. I'm glad he sent it. But I always wondered why you never showed up."

"I couldn't find you. I did not know where I was going as an eight-year-old on the streets. My mother told me you worked somewhere in the City of London, it's a big place for a young boy." Jack crossed his arms across his chest.

"Jack, listen to me. Cecil moved in closer. "I'm not apportioning blame, I just wondered where you were. I kept a look outside my shop. I stepped outside three times a day in case you came by without realising I was here.

Jack gazed towards the floor. "Does this mean that you believe you are my uncle, then? You don't think I'm lying do you?"

"Oh, Jack. I knew who you were the moment you walked in. You have your mother's eyes."

"My ma. How is she? I have to see her. Let's see if we can get in touch with her. It will make her overjoyed to know I have found you."

Oliver coughed.

"Shh, they don't know we're listening in," Clara whispered, putting her finger to her mouth.

Oliver rolled his eyes, looked away, and put his ear against the door. Cecil glanced at the door but chose to ignore the sound.

"I'm so sorry, Jack."

"What is it? Why do you look so sad?"

Cecil's eyes began to water. "Your mother died about four years ago. It was a terrible accident. She banged her head and never woke up."

Jack's tears fell from the corners of his eyes, his cheeks turned a mottled pink.

"Jack?" Cecil ducked his head slightly to try to lock eyes with his nephew. "There is something else."

"What's that?"

"Your father is dead, too. He took his own life. I'm sorry, Jack," he said, moving towards his nephew to embrace him.

"I don't believe it, I just don't." Jack broke free from his uncle. He sat on the wooden stool in the corner, leaning forward with his head in his hands.

"I'm so sorry to have to tell you that. I don't know how close you were to them. Regardless, hearing your parents have died is grief beyond measure."

Jack was quiet for a few moments, then he wiped his tears away with his shirt sleeve. It left visible damp trails on the cotton almost making the material transparent.

"It feels like I have been on a never-ending journey. Not just to find you. But I hoped that one day it would reunite me with my ma in particular. I was hesitant to see pa after what he did to ma."

"Some people go through difficult times. We can't forgive them for their behaviour, but we can have compassion."

"I know. And besides, I'm not completely without a family am I?"

"No, you're not. You have me."

"I need to go and tell Clara." Jack stood up from the stool and walked towards the door.

"I don't think you'll need to."

"Why?"

"I have a feeling she has been listening to every word." Cecil raised his eyebrows towards the door.

Jack turned the handle and saw two faces close together.

Clara and Oliver moved quickly and shuffled their way to the front of the shop.

"It's okay, you don't have to pretend you heard nothing," Jack said.

"Sorry, I couldn't help myself. I know how important this is to you."

"Clara, go home for the rest of the day. I think we will be quiet anyway, so Oliver and I can cover the shop. Take Jack with you and keep each other company."

"Only if you're sure, Mr Dalton?"

"Yes, I'm quite sure. It's been an eventful morning and I think Jack could do with a close friend. Isn't that right, Jack?"

Jack smiled admirably at Cecil. "Thank you, uncle, thank you so much."

As Clara and Jack stepped outside, they almost bumped into the gentleman who had come to collect his suits.

"Leo! Sorry, Mr Cooper, have you come to collect your suits?"

"Clara, my good friend. Yes, are they ready? And who is this?" he said, looking in Jack's direction.

"My uncle will see you. This is my friend, Jack. He sings, you know?"

"Does he? Perhaps he would like to audition one day," Leo stepped into the shop and left Jack and Clara with his intriguing parting invitation.

Jack and Clara travelled back to Holly village in the black, shiny Brougham carriage. They talked about the remarkable discovery of his uncle all the way home. Jack smiled as he spoke fondly about his uncle and, thanked Clara for telling him about how she thought her new employer could be his uncle.

"I will be forever grateful to you, Clara."

"I know," she said, reaching for his hand.

But little did Jack know that what he was about to see would change his life forever.

Chapter 22

"I can't wait to tell Isabella and William, Clara, I'm so excited."

Clara had never seen her friend looking so happy. "It's such great news. I'm sure my father will be pleased, too. He knew what it meant to you to find your uncle."

"Before anything else, let's tell your father." He has been so kind to me over the years."

"You're so considerate, Jack."

"I haven't forgotten who threw me those pennies when I was homeless. He doesn't know how much they mattered."

"I'm sure he understands. He prefers not to see anyone on the streets, especially in winter."

Isabella was at the Walker's house. She had been keeping herself amused all morning with the new stable hand. He was tall and handsome and new to the Walker family, and Isabella couldn't resist. With blond curls, dark brown eyes, and a cheeky grin, it was hard not to fall for him.

"Clarence, you are so funny!" Isabella said with a laugh. "How did you become so handsome?"

"Steady on, Isabella, you are engaged!"

"I wouldn't quite go that far. I'm not sure Jack loves me that much anymore. He humiliated me last night at dinner, so I thought I would look for alternative entertainment." She pushed Clarence backwards onto the bales of hay, then hitched the trusses of her dress up and fell on top of him. "Don't worry, I won't say a word. Jack isn't back from London for hours yet!"

"Isabella, please get off me, I'm not that kind of man. I don't want to be on the receiving end of your advances when you are engaged to someone else." Clarence fumbled and wrestled with Isabella's hands. He tried to push the hems of her skirts back towards her ankles, whilst juggling keeping her hands away from his buckle. "Isabella! Please!"

Isabella ignored him, her lips kissing his neck with her hands now battling with the buttons on his shirt. Her heart paced faster, and she felt the tiny hairs on her skin give her tingles and stand on end.

Jack and Clara stepped out of the carriage and ran up the steps leading to the front door of George's house. Jack couldn't wait to spread his good news.

"That is just wonderful. You must have mixed emotions though, being thrilled to have found your uncle yet grief-stricken at the news of your parents." George sat on the sofa in the drawing room. The good news caused celebration, and he poured him and Jack a whisky, and a sherry for Clara.

"It's not five o'clock yet, father."

"It doesn't matter," he said, holding the crystal cut glass up to the light to reflect on the amber liquid. "This is a one-off. And for good reason." He gave his daughter a sympathetic smile, knowing that drinking in the daytime brought back memories of her mother that they would both rather forget.

"My mother will finally be at peace, but my thoughts on my father remain unsaid."

The young woman felt emotionless when her mother died. With the passing years, Esther's existence became forgotten.

"I'm very pleased for you."

"Thank you, but please excuse me while I go and tell Isabella. I will be back shortly and maybe we can have another drink together."

"That would be wonderful."

George looked at his daughter and couldn't help but notice how smitten his daughter was with Jack.

Jack left the Cavendish's house and happily made his way back to the Walkers. He couldn't wait to tell Isabella. Despite the tension after last night, he hoped the news would improve his feelings towards his fiancé.

"Isabella. Isabella?" Jack walked through the stables and past the horses.

"Shh, don't let him hear you." Isabella's face touched Clarence's, she held a finger to her lips begging him to not say a word.

Clarence thought his heart was going to burst through his chest. Looking up at the roof of the stables, he prayed.

"Isabella?" Jack walked to the back of the stables. It was their favourite place they shared when they wanted private time.

Jack turned the corner and walked past the empty stable at the end, almost missing the two bodies on the hay bales. He took three steps back having registered somewhere in his mind the two horizontal figures. He gulped, and it hurt his throat. His eyes slowly began to glaze over. "What's happening here?"

Clarence and Isabella looked up. Their cheeks blushed, and Clarence's eyes darted to the side instead of focusing on the man in front of him.

"Jack, hi. Erm, this—this is Clarence."

"Is it now? It looks to me like you are getting very friendly with Clarence, so I will leave you to it." Jack turned on his heels and started walking away.

"Please, don't be like that. I thought you didn't love me after last night." Isabella stood up and ran after Jack. She caught up with him and grabbed hold of his elbow, trying to turn him around.

Jack shrugged her off. "Don't be so selfish, Isabella, it's not all about you, you know."

"What do you mean?"

"It doesn't matter. I'm not spending my life with somebody so flippant. We're finished."

"Jack!"

Chapter 23

"You seem like you had a rough night, Jack," George remarked, eyeing the man before him. Dark circles under his eyes and ruffled hair made him look ten years older.

Jack raised his eyebrows and let out a breath. "I think I did. Anything to drown my sorrows and take my mind off Isabella."

"Did you get any sleep?"

"Not really. I tossed and turned all night. I can't help but think what a fool I've been. Getting engaged to her was a mistake. She was always the mischievous one. But I never thought she would betray me. Particularly after everything I've done for her."

"Women are complicated sometimes, Jack. What do you think you'll do?"

Jack shrugged his shoulders. "I don't think I want to marry her now. If she can be deceitful now, what will she be like as a wife?"

"Aren't you going to talk to her about yesterday?"

"No, I've made my mind up," he said, lifting his chin slightly.

"As long as you're sure. I think you're taking the easy way out because you have someone else on your mind. Isabella has given you an excuse to end the relationship, but she probably didn't mean what she did."

Jack brought his fist up to his mouth and cleared his throat. "I don't know what you're talking about. There is no one else."

"Good morning."

George noticed Jack's eyes light up as Clara walked into the room. Jack saw George's glance and looked away quickly, not noticing George's raised eyebrows.

"Morning," Jack grunted.

"You don't sound very happy, are you okay?"

"He has a headache after last night, ignore him."

"That's to be expected. I left him as he dozed off with a whisky in his hand, around midnight." Clara said, shaking her head.

"I am here and hearing your every word."

Clara rolled her eyes at her father, then busied herself buttering toast and drinking coffee.

"Jack, it's heartbreaking for men too when something like that happens. We don't expect our partners to be disloyal, we think we will be with them forever, but then suddenly our futures change because of one stupid mistake."

"I never expected her to do that to me. I thought we had something special, but it seems we didn't."

Clara coughed a little and held her coffee cup in both hands. "Correction, Jack. You did have something special. It seems like she was unfaithful for the first time as a way of getting back at you out of anger and jealousy from your conversation the previous night. It would have been better for her to communicate her feelings to you, instead of going behind your back and rolling around in the hay with another man."

"Either way, there is no future for us." Jack didn't notice Clara who tried desperately not to smile.

"What will you do for work? You can't continue working there after what's happened, can you?"

"I had a long think about things last night. I would be devastated if I failed the Walkers after their years of kindness."

"They have been so kind and generous to you, but you also need to move on. Have you considered living with your uncle?" George said.

"I would have to find new work. I couldn't travel every day." Jack threw his serviette down in frustration. Isabella's infidelity caused all of this to happen."

"I think you would have separated, anyway. I'm not sure you were suited to each other. Besides, you could live with your uncle now and get to know him better. You could still work at the Walkers. Why don't you travel to and from the house with me? The groomsman can bring you to the Walkers after he has taken me to the shop, then he could bring you back when he comes and collects me."

"You have an answer for everything don't you?"

Clara stood up, walked over to Jack, and touched his nose. "Yes, I do, and I'm proud of it," she said, smiling.

"Are you not finishing your breakfast?" George shouted after his daughter.

"Not hungry, father!" She called, as she walked off to get her coat.

George looked at Jack and rolled his eyes. "That young lady is so independent."

"Yes, but it suits her." Jack's eyes followed Clara out of the room. When he turned his gaze back to the room, he caught George grinning at him.

"Sure there's no one else on your mind?"

Jack stood up and walked out of the dining room, avoiding the conversation that would admit his desire to marry Clara.

Chapter 24

᎗᎒᎗᎒᎗✦᎒᎗᎒᎗

"Clara, what would happen if I went to live with my uncle? Will we still see each other?"

"Of course, we would, silly. As often as we make time for. How do you feel about Isabella?"

"I thought she was the one, but I was so young when I met her. I guess you grow into someone don't you rather than being attracted to them. But I don't want to be with someone I can't trust."

"Trust is an important part of any relationship. If you can't trust someone, what's the point?'

Jack nodded his head. "I know, and she has broken mine."

"You'll have to talk to her, eventually. I don't like what she's done, but she deserves to know that you can't marry her."

"It will be difficult to have that conversation without upsetting the Walkers."

"I think they'll understand. It seems to me they have known what she's like ever since she went to live with them."

"Perhaps."

"Anyway, no time to continue this conversation. You need to talk to your uncle about living with him."

They both stepped out of the carriage and walked into the shop. The brass bell above the door rang out.

"Morning, Oliver."

"Morning Clara, morning Jack." The second greeting wasn't quite as chirpy as the first.

"Where is Mr Dalton?"

"He's searching the storeroom for the perfect material for Leo's costume."

"Costume? Who will that be for?"

"Nancy, she is starring in the opening night of The Willow Copse next Friday so it needs to be perfect."

"I thought I heard voices. It's good to see you again, Jack." Cecil walked through to the shop, his thin gold-rimmed spectacles hanging at the end of his nose and a measuring tape was around his neck.

"Morning uncle," I don't think I will ever get used to saying that."

"Is everything alright with you? You seem rather glum." Cecil gazed down through the spectacles at the end of his nose and raised his eyebrows whilst he cut the rose pink velvet.

"Not really. I was so excited about telling Isabella yesterday that I had found you. That good feeling was ruined when I found her with another man in the stables."

"Ah, you won't be happy about that then. I'm assuming Isabella is your fiancé."

"I never told you yesterday."

"I am sorry to hear that. What are you going to do?"

"I'm not sure, that's why I've come to speak to you. There are so many things to consider. I'm not sure I can continue working at the stables, then where do I live? I would feel uncomfortable continuing to live at the Walkers."

"I would love to have you living with me, it would be great."

"Thank you, but what would I do for work?"

"I can't help on that front I'm afraid. I have Oliver and Clara here, no need for anyone else right now."

"I have said he can continue to travel with me, Mr Dalton, until he finds alternative work. I think it's the ideal solution, don't you? My groomsman will bring me here while Jack can return with him to work at the Walkers, and vice versa. A perfect solution, don't you think?"

"That would seem to solve the problem temporarily, doesn't it?"

"Yes, it does."

"Marvellous! If you're here all day, you can help Oliver move the new material into the back of the shop."

"I have to return to Holly village for a final Christmas concert by the cross in the square. I hope to start at six o'clock."

"That's okay, you will be finished in plenty of time."

It was late morning and Jack was helping Oliver whilst singing Christmas carols and practicing for that evening.

"Do you not think it's a bit late to be singing carols?" Oliver said.

"What do you mean? There is nothing like the Christmas spirit, and what's wrong with me singing them?"

"You're a young man, Jack, men don't sing, not where I come from, anyway. We leave it to the ladies."

"I think it's good to have a mix of voices, there is nothing wrong with it in my view."

"Well, I think you're weak."

"Weak? That's a bit unfair, you hardly know me."

"Clara wants a real man in her life, regardless. Not one that works in stables and sings carols. She wants someone who can support and satisfy her, and you're not that person."

"I never said I was, but I doubt you are either."

"I'm determined to marry Clara, and there's no stopping it."

"Let's allow Clara to decide whether she marries you or not. You don't even know her!"

"Why are you so protective of her?"

"I'm not, I'm just saying you hardly know her so why think about marriage?"

"Because I like her and have my mind set on courting her. There's nothing you can do about it either."

"We'll see about that!"

"Jack! Will you come here?" Cecil shouted.

Jack walked through to the shop front, gazing towards the floor. "What is it, uncle?" he said without looking up.

Cecil nodded and raised his eyebrows at a woman behind the counter.

"Isabella, what are you doing here?"

"I came to talk to you seeing that you're ignoring me."

"I'm not, I'm just—busy."

"Jack, why don't you take a walk, we can manage here," Cecil said.

"Where's Clara gone? Can you manage with just two people?"

"Clara will be back shortly. She has gone to see a supplier for me."

Jack led Isabella out of the shop and down the street.

"Isabella, let's not waste time and fool around. I can't be with you anymore. I was rude to you and you've been unfaithful. That's not great, is it before we are even married?"

"I haven't been unfaithful, Jack," she said, trying to reach for his hand.

He shrugged his arm away from her. "Isabella, regardless of what happened, you intended to kiss that man. It's only because I caught you that you stopped."

"That's not true, Jack!" she said stamping her feet, tears forming in her eyes.

"It is, and you know it. I'm sorry Isabella, I won't be taken for a fool."

"It's all because of your love for Clara."

"I'm not in love with her, she's a friend. I wouldn't have asked you to marry me if I was in love with someone else."

"You're a liar, Jack. A liar."

Jack shook his head, turned around, and started walking back to the shop, leaving a distraught Isabella crying in the street.

Chapter 25

I sabella ran after the only man she had ever loved. She wasn't willing to give him up that easily.

"Jack, Jack, please wait." With tears dribbling down her face, she looked a mess. Her cheeks were mottled pink and her hair was looking more bedraggled every minute as a result of the snow that began to fall.

"Please, Jack, don't leave me."

Jack came to a halt. He put his hands on his hips, sighed deeply, then turned around. He closed his eyes briefly and shook his head. "I can't Isabella, I just can't. I won't be able to trust you ever again and I can't marry you when there is no trust."

"But, Jack, you are everything to me. What will I do without you?"

"I don't care."

Isabella reached out and wrapped her arms around Jack's waist. She rested her head against his chest and sobbed her heart out.

Chapter 26

"You look very happy today, Clara. Has something put a smile on your face?"

"Maybe," she said, her eyes looking up and down at the eclectic colours and textures of material. The rolls of fabric were lined up neatly on the dark wood shelves in the warehouse. Bright feathers, beads and ribbon were stored in a cupboard to the right hand side of the shelves.

"Is it a man by any chance?"

"Do you normally ask your customers such personal questions Mr Hargreaves?"

The material supplier blushed and busied himself unpacking more fabric.

"I didn't mean to embarrass you, Mr Hargreaves. I was just teasing. I am in love and I think he is too."

"That's marvelous, when is the big day?"

"Big day?"

"Yes, your wedding."

"We are not quite at that stage yet. We aren't even courting."

"What's a few weeks amongst friends? If you like him and the feeling is mutual, I don't know what you are waiting around for."

Clara brought a finger up to her lips and pondered what he said. "Do you know, I think you might be right. I have somewhere to go, I will see you later." Clara dashed out of the warehouse and started to make her way back to Mr Dalton's tailors. Her footsteps were light and she hummed to herself. *I must tell Jack how I feel. Mr Hargreaves is right, why wait.*

Clara turned the corner onto Back Street and imagined what she was going to say to Jack. She had known for a while that she wanted to marry him, it's only Isabella who had got in the way.

The young woman looked up when she heard a commotion in the street. After recognising who it was doing the shouting, her blood ran cold and her eyes began to water. Her skin felt a chill and she wondered how she could have been so stupid.

The couple on the other side of the street were close together and it looked as if they weren't going to break free from each other any time soon.

You fool, Clara, you fool.

"Isabella, stop this. I can't be with you. I don't want you anymore." Jack unwrapped her arms from around his waist and walked away back to his uncle's store.

Oliver quickly moved away from the window leaving a facial imprint on the steamed glass. He wiped it away quickly with his forearm then continued sorting the material in the back room.

The door opened and let in a gush of cold air. "Oliver, have you finished tidying up those rolls of material yet?"

Oliver frowned. "Has something upset you? You left very happy this morning before you went to see Mr Hargreaves."

"I'm fine."

Oliver raised his eyebrows and continued with his work.

"Jack, there you are. Did you chat to Isabella?" Cecil said.

"Yes, but I don't want to discuss it."

"Is it your embrace you don't want to discuss, Jack?" Oliver whispered when Jack joined him in the store room.

"Shut up, and keep your nose out of my business."

"I told you that Clara is all mine. Why don't you run back to Isabella and leave me to marry Clara?"

Cecil pouted at Clara, raising his eyebrows. His spectacles slipped towards the end of his nose.

Clara stood with her hands on her hips, listening to the conversation.

"Clara will never marry you. You're not good enough for her."

"Stop it! Have you heard the pair of you?"

Jack and Oliver dropped what they were holding, making a clattering sound on the wooden floor.

"I will choose who I marry and when. Why don't you just get on with what you are doing. And as for you, Jack. I saw you with Isabella. Clearly you feel very differently to me than I do with you."

Clara walked out of the shop with tears in her eyes.

"Clara! Clara! Wait."

But it was too late. She walked away and didn't look back.

Chapter 27

Jack sang and played to the crowd like he did every Christmas. But his mind was elsewhere. Faces young and old smiled at him. Flakes of snow covering their winter clothes. He wasn't interested in any of them except the couple at the back. Clara and Oliver stood by the Oak tree, capturing his attention. He noticed Oliver reach for Clara's hand and she returned the gesture.

George looked at Jack, then back at his daughter and Oliver. He gave his daughter's lifelong friend a nonchalant smile.

The sound of laughter and cheery voices should have brought a festive smile to Jack's face. Usually excited this time of year, he expected this to be his best Christmas yet, especially after being reunited with his uncle.

But Jack had doom and gloom spread across his face.

"Jack, you'll be okay. I'm not sure what has happened between you and Clara, but I know she will come round."

"I doubt it, George. She has chosen to be with him. I guess I will be spending Christmas without you both this year. I had hoped it would be one of my happiest Christmases." Jack looked up at George, then noticed Clara and Oliver walking hand in hand along the cobbled street, away from the village square.

"If it's any consolation, Jack, I don't think he's right for her. He's too creepy." He patted Jack's back, then followed his daughter back to the house.

Jack said goodnight to some villagers and wished them a happy Christmas. He tried to appear joyful and festive, but internally, devastation consumed every cell in his body. He walked to catch the omnibus back to the city. He wouldn't be going to George and Clara's tonight.

He walked along the cobbled street, to where the omnibus would pick him up. He noticed that most of the crowd had now disappeared, it must be at least an hour since he finished singing. In the dim light, he took each step with care. His mind was on Clara and Isabella, and his gaze was on the slippery cobbles below. He relied on the lantern that he was carrying with him to light his path ahead. Trees flanked the road, looming over him, the pickup point was at least five minutes away.

His mind was elsewhere, and he was humming to himself. Suddenly, he felt a weight on his back. It almost pushed him to the ground. *What the—* A kick to his legs made his knees almost buckle. "What do you want with me? Why are you doing this?" Jack said, struggling for breath. He fell backwards onto the frozen ground when the figure lurking behind him moved to the front and pushed him over. The man sat on top of his chest and Jack saw a fist flying towards his face. "Who are you? Why are you—? Oliver? Is that—"

"Oliver, you are being dramatic. I have told you already I've not even thought about marrying Clara!"

"Don't lie to me, why don't you just leave the village, no one wants you around here, not even Isabella."

"Oliver stop it!" Jack suddenly felt rage for the first time in years. Maybe it was all the anger coming out of him after hearing about his parents' death. "Leave me alone and grow up. Well-respected men don't fight. Change your ways if you want a chance with Clara."

Jack took the slight hesitation and loss of grip from Oliver as a chance to move. He pushed Oliver to the side, rolled over, and stood up. " Leave me alone, Oliver! You don't know anything about me!" he said as he brushed himself down. "You're pathetic, you don't deserve Clara or anyone else like her, you are nothing but trouble. I knew it the first time I set eyes on you. Now go home."

Jack walked off leaving Oliver on the ground. *Today couldn't get worse, it feels like everyone is against me.*

Jack walked down the road, physically and emotionally wounded. He made his way to his uncle's house, fed up with the situation. Rather than catch the omnibus, he chose to walk home to clear his head and think about his future, but regretted it now. His fingers and toes felt like ice and his ripped coat let in the freezing cold temperatures of the night.

"Jack, what on earth has happened?" Cecil's mouth was open wide at Jack standing in front of him like a broken man. "Come in, come on, don't just stand there, it's freezing outside." Jack entered his uncle's sitting room and immediately felt himself relax in front of the fire. He sat forward and put his hands in front of the flames and rubbed them together.

"Here, drink this," Cecil said, passing him a brandy.

Jack drank the dark golden liquid back in three gulps. His nerves slowly started to steady and his hands stopped shaking.

"Are you going to tell me what's happened?"

"You won't believe me."

"Try me, Jack, I'm here for you."

Jack sighed and looked up at his uncle. "Oliver beat me up."

"Oliver?"

"Yes, Oliver."

"Are you—are you quite sure?"

"Yes, he sat on top of my chest and nearly thumped my jaw. It was definitely him. I knew he was trouble the first time I met him."

"I'm surprised, I didn't think he was like that."

"I guess he will do anything to get the woman he wants."

"This isn't over Clara, is it?"

Jack remained in his seat, wordlessly gazing at his uncle.

"She is a wonderful woman I suppose. I haven't met anybody as remarkable as her in at least ten years.

"Why ten?"

"Elsie, my wife. She died years ago, but I've not once forgotten her." Cecil stared straight ahead at the flames.

"I'm sorry to hear that, uncle Cecil. You must have been very happy together."

"We were. She was wonderful. But since her death I've made many friends, so I'm not all that lonely. Anyway, let's get you cleaned up." Cecil walked to the kitchen to get a bowl of warm water, gauze, and Iodine to clean his nephew's wounds.

After soothing Jack's cuts and bruises with some warm water, the two gentlemen sat near the fire and drank more brandy.

"Where is Oliver now?"

"I do not know and I don't care, but I won't be returning to the Walkers. I don't think I will be seeing Clara again, either. In fact, I probably shouldn't be anywhere near your shop tomorrow. I'm likely to hit him."

"No you won't. First thing tomorrow, I'll be showing him the door. He doesn't do that to anybody, least of all family."

There was a brief silence between the two men.

"What's on your mind?"

"I'm just thinking," Cecil said, tilting his glass against the light before taking another sip.

"What's that?"

"How can we separate Oliver from Clara?"

"I don't think you'll be able to, it's like he's obsessed with her. Besides, she won't come near me. She caught me and Isabella together yesterday."

"Is that why she was in a mood when she returned from Mr Hargreaves?"

"I imagine so."

"And are you with Isabella?"

"No, far from it. She grabbed hold of me in the street and Clara got the wrong impression."

"We'll have to fix that then won't we?"

Jack looked at his uncle. "You'll be lucky. I think I've lost her forever." Jack knocked his brandy back in one final gulp, slammed the glass down on the table and sighed deeply.

Chapter 28

J ack stood on the doorstep of the Walker's house shifting from foot to foot. He gazed at the sky, pondering how to break the news to William.

"Jack, what has happened? Look at the state of you." William looked up and down at his friend, then focused on the cuts and bruises on his face.

"It's a bit complicated."

"Come on in and tell me everything."

William led Jack through to the welcoming drawing room. The fire was lit providing a warmth against the chill outside. The Christmas tree still stood in the corner adorned with decorations of oranges, cloves, and cinnamon sticks.

The two men sat opposite each other. Jack leaned forward and put his elbows on his knees, his hands clasped in front of him.

"Have you seen Clara today?"

"Briefly. She called this morning to introduce us to her beau. He's a bit odd if you ask me. But, Clara seems to like him and that's all that matters."

"He's not a nice person. We have to help get her away from him before he hurts her, too."

"Don't tell me Oliver did this to you?"

Jack nodded, then gulped down his emotion.

"He's jealous of what Clara and I shared, or used to share. He thought in his wisdom that beating me up would keep me away from her. It was a mindless act and one that hurt."

"Does Clara know?"

"No, you can't tell her."

"I can, she must know."

"She will think I'm making it up."

"Why would she think that?"

"To make her have sympathy I suppose."

"You're not making any sense Jack, what has gone on here?"

"I take it you heard what happened with me and Isabella?"

"I did. She is distraught, Jack."

"Distraught? But she is the one that messed it up!" Jack raised his voice.

"She still loves you, regardless."

"I find that hard to believe. You can't trust someone when they go behind your back."

"I don't think she meant it, Jack. She was hurting from your argument with her the night before. Perhaps she just wanted to make you jealous to teach you a lesson."

"What lesson would that be?"

"To be nice to her and give her more attention. You are the best thing that's ever happened to her, but she's worried you are in love with Clara."

"I—"

"Yes, Jack?"

"Oh, it doesn't matter. The whole situation is a mess and one that won't be resolved soon."

"The only thing I can do is tell Clara what Oliver has done. She doesn't deserve someone like that after what she went through with her mother."

"I know. But I don't think she will listen to you. I suppose you have more of a chance of talking to her than I do though."

"Leave it to me, Jack. I will see what I can do. You must decide who you want to be with. It's not fair on Clara or Isabella if you keep them both guessing."

"I've always held a flame for Clara."

"We know that. That's why I was surprised to hear about you and Isabella."

"We fell into each other, William. We were friends and grew into something different as we got older. But then—"

William raised his eyebrows at his friend.

"I realised that I wanted Clara, and now I feel terribly guilty."

"The guilt will fade once you decide. Isabella never was the one for you. You could do so much better for yourself. I know I am related to Isabella and whilst she has calmed down, she is nothing but trouble."

"Perhaps her and Oliver would be well suited together."

"Maybe so. But that doesn't solve the problem of your lodgings and work, does it? You are more than welcome to continue staying with us Jack. I'm just not sure whether it is a good idea."

"I came to speak with you about that. My uncle has offered for me to stay with him for the unforeseeable future. I feel like I have found my family again after everything that has happened."

"And what about work? Do you want to keep working in the stables here? We would miss you if you went. The Walkers and I fell lucky with you working for us. It would be a shame if you had to leave."

"I will keep working for you in the short term if that's alright with you? I don't know how long I will last, but at least I will be earning something whilst I look for work elsewhere. The situation isn't ideal, especially with Isabella living here and Clara next door. But it is what it is for now."

"Things will work out, Jack. I promise."

Isabella heard voices as she reached the bottom of the stairs. She was on her way to join her grandmother for afternoon tea. The conversation made her stop and listen some more. She stood outside the door and her heart sank. She desperately wanted to be with Jack, but knew she had ruined her chances. Still, she felt she should give it one last go.

"Jack, I'm so pleased to see you."

Jack looked up, his expression was one of anger.

"I am so sorry about what happened between us. Is there any chance for us?"

"I'm sorry, Isabella, I'm just not interested. I don't want to experience any more heartache. I have told William that I am moving in with my uncle. I'll stay working here for now, but leave once I find something else."

"But—Jack. Please, can we not talk about this?"

Jack stood up, shook his head, and silently walked away in disgust. He didn't give Isabella a second chance, that part of his life was over now.

"You can hardly blame him can you, Isabella? "He has helped keep you on the straight and narrow and you repay him by lifting your dress at the first sign of him not meeting your expectations."

Isabella felt sorry for herself, she loved Jack. She was jealous of the friendship between Clara and Jack and had been ever since she met them both. But her reckless behaviour and trying to hide it from Jack, had only made him move on. Her plans to make him jealous had backfired.

"You look sad, Isabella."

"I am. I thought I had a future with him."

"Maybe you did, but not anymore. If you want a good, honest husband, here's my advice. Grow up and treat people with respect or you won't get anywhere in life." William shook his head and walked out wondering what the future held for her.

Chapter 29

"You haven't heard, have you?"

Clara bit her lip and glanced around the shop. "What am I supposed to have heard? Am I missing out on something?"

Cecil raised his eyebrows.

"And where's Oliver this morning? Is he late?" she said, looking around for her beau and colleague.

"I'm surprised you don't know where Oliver is."

Clara's cheeks flushed at the assumption.

"I'm sorry, maybe that was uncalled for."

"Yes, it was. Have I upset you in any way?"

"No, you haven't, but Oliver has."

"What has he done? It can't be that bad."

"It is, I'm afraid. Have you seen Jack this morning?"

"No. The coachman waited for him after I arrived here, but he didn't show up.

"Hmm. He told me he would walk to work this morning, so I'm not surprised."

"Are you going to tell me what's wrong, or keep me guessing?"

"Oliver beat Jack up last night." Cecil waited for Clara's response.

Clara shook her head in denial. " He wouldn't do that. He was with me."

"Until what time?"

"He left as soon as he had walked me back to the house after the Christmas Carol concert. Father wasn't keen on inviting him in, so he left."

"I'm not surprised. I'm sorry to say, Clara, that it happened around eight thirty when Jack was on his way back to mine. He turned up in a right state."

Clara's heart sank. She gazed towards the floor without saying a word.

"I know it's difficult for you to hear, Clara, but Oliver is not a pleasant man to be with."

"Neither is Jack," she retorted. " Oliver may not be perfect, but did Jack tell you what happened between him and Isabella?"

"He said he didn't want to see her anymore, but she persisted."

Clara frowned. "But I saw them hugging each other."

"Yes, they did. Jack told me. But he had every right to. It's not as if you are engaged to him."

"I know that, but—but I had feelings for him. And I thought he did for me. I was wrong."

"You're not wrong, Clara. But you read the situation wrong with him and Isabella on the street. When Jack walked away, Isabella chased after him and wouldn't let him go. You probably caught the tail end of the argument."

Clara brought her hand to her lips.

Cecil sighed and walked towards her, noticing that her eyes had watered. "It's not too late to change your mind, Clara. Jack still desperately wants you, but he thinks he has ruined his chances with you. And as for Oliver ..."

"I must go and find him. I regret holding Oliver's hand now and going to the concert with him. I suppose I just wanted to make Jack jealous."

"It appears Jack is in high demand then, doesn't it? Isabella shared the same jealous intention by rolling in the hay with Clarence".

"Oh, God, Cecil. What have I done?" Clara brought her hands to her cheeks.

"Don't worry about that now. Find Jack and tell him how you feel. But be quick. He told me he was leaving tonight to go and pay his respects to his parents. He won't be back for a few days."

Clara turned on her heels and glanced back once before leaving.

"Go on, go. I can manage here."

She didn't need telling twice.

With no time to wait for the carriage, Clara picked up the trusses of her skirts and ran all the way to the Walkers.

Chapter 30

FIVE YEARS LATER

"I will marry you when you decide to pursue your career in the theatre. You know it's meant to be. Every time Leo from the Adelphi comes to the shop, he asks you to audition. He has heard you singing in the background frequently. And he simply wouldn't ask if he didn't think you weren't good enough. He is highly ranked in the theatre world, it could be your lucky break."

"I'm just not sure it's for me, Clara. I am quite happy singing at Christmas time with you by my side. It is a small audience, so no pressure."

"But, Jack, you would earn so much more money if your uncle doesn't mind what I'm saying."

"Of course not. But maybe I should give you a pay rise, so you stay," Cecil said, rolling his eyes. "Look, Jack, you have to think of your future. Whilst I enjoy having you here, as I am sure Clara does, you have to have aspirations. Clara is right. Mr Cooper has repeatedly asked you to audition, but without success."

"I'm not sure it's for me," Jack said, singing his way to the back room. He didn't hear the bell above the door ring at the front of the shop.

"Hello, Leo, how are you today?"

"Jack is singing again I hear. Have you convinced him to join us at the theatre?"

"Not quite, no. But let's get you measured up in the meantime, shall we?"

"I have an idea." Leo beckoned Clara and Cecil closer with his hand.

They huddled their heads together and waited for Leo to speak.

"Nancy is performing in the new theatre tonight. It's the opening night after that dreadful fire. Her husband and daughter will be there too. If I give you tickets, you could come along and speak to her before the performance. Maybe she will be accommodating to Jack auditioning." Leo raised his eyebrows.

Clara and Cecil looked at each other.

"How many tickets do you have?"

"I can get you three. I will drop them here later and give them to you."

"Could you stretch to four? I would love to bring my father." Clara's eyes twinkled. It was hard for any man to resist, even Leo who was the other way inclined.

"Of course. I assume he approves of Jack auditioning too?"

"He does, he's trying to encourage him."

"I suppose he only wants what's best for his daughter."

Clara had a glint in her eye. "He does, particularly if Jack and I are going to get married."

"That's exciting. When is the special day?" Leo said as he followed Cecil towards the back room to get measured.

"Never if Jack doesn't audition."

"Well, we can't have that. Let's see what happens later."

"Sounds perfect," Clara said.

"What have I missed? Did I hear you talking about me?" Jack said as he emerged from the store room.

"Nothing. But be prepared to go out tonight. We're off to see a show," Clara said, tapping Jack's nose and continuing her work with a grin.

Chapter 31

"**A**re you looking forward to the show, father?"

"It's impromptu, put it that way. I was planning on having an early evening."

"Leo put in a lot of effort to ensure you got a ticket."

"It's not that I'm ungrateful, Clara. Like I say, I was going to retire early."

"Father, this is your daughter's future at stake. You want Jack to audition as badly as I do, don't you? You know he'll be successful when he finally stars in a show. It's just a matter of a bit more encouragement."

"Are you talking about me again behind my back?" Jack walked up to Clara and kissed her gently on the cheek.

"No, just plotting."

"As long as your plot has a happy ending, that's all I'm bothered about." Jack took a step back and admired his sweetheart standing in front of him. "How do you always look so beautiful?"

"It comes natural to me," Clara said, fluttering her eyelashes. "Are you almost ready, father?" Clara turned her attention back to the man she loved unconditionally.

"Why don't you two go ahead, I won't be far behind."

"As long as you are coming?" Clara waited for an answer.

"Yes, of course I will be."

Jack shrugged his shoulders, then led Clara out of the house. "Look, it's so pretty up there." Jack pointed to the sky.

"It is, but it's not snowing."

"That doesn't matter, the stars are shining brightly. It's a beautiful, clear evening. Why don't we walk a little and your father can pick us up in the carriage as he passes?"

Clara smiled and reached out for Jack's hand.

"I am looking forward to Christmas this year, Jack. I'm also hoping it will be our last before we are married."

Jack's stomach felt like it had flipped over. When will he ever find the courage to ask her to marry him again? Being turned down three times was enough to damage anybody's confidence.

"I would love to propose again, Clara, but you keep turning me down."

"My father wants to make sure you can provide for me."

"I love you. What more does he want?"

"You know what he wants, what we both want for you. Audition properly for shows, Jack. You know you will be good."

"Maybe so, but I don't know if it's really me. We've spoken about this before. Besides, how will it give you what your father's looking for?"

"Because you know damn well that you will earn more money. It's good working together with your uncle, but it doesn't pay much, he said so himself."

"Since you work there too, what's the problem?"

"It's different for me, Jack. I love it, and I don't need the money. You belong on the stage, that's your genuine passion, I know it is."

"I guess you're right, as always," he sighed.

"There, see. More enthusiasm will give you all the confidence you need. When you watch the show tonight, imagine being up there in the lights. I think it will surprise you how much it will make you smile."

"You make me smile, Clara Cavendish." Jack turned to her and kissed her gently on the lips.

"Jack, don't let anyone see us, we're not married."

"No, but we soon will be. Besides, no one is looking, and it's none of their business."

Jack and Clara leaned in closer to each other and embraced tightly under the moonlit sky. They clung to each other, oblivious to their surroundings until they heard a voice.

"Well, well, who do we have here?"

Jack and Clara froze, all four cheeks turning pink, and their eyes widened. Their lips unlocked and they slowly unfurled themselves from each other.

"I haven't seen you for a year Jack, how are you?" The heavily pregnant woman blanked Clara.

"I'm well, thank you, Isabella, and you?"

"Yes, I'm well thank you. As you can see, I am expecting my first child very soon."

"So you are, well you have a good Christmas and give my regards to your Uncle William."

"I will, Jack. And a Merry Christmas to you too."

Clara and Jack walked tentatively on the slippery cobbles away from Isabella.

Clara rolled her eyes. "She doesn't change much, does she?"

"Isabella seems to have turned a corner with her politeness," Jack said as he walked by Clara's side.

"I wouldn't quite go that far, she completely ignored me."

"Well, don't be upset, darling, you deserve better people to speak to."

"Oh, and Clara?"

They both turned around to see Isabella hadn't walked another step. She stood on the spot, staring at the couple.

"I've never forgiven you for stealing him from me, just so you know." Isabella gave a cold, hard stare.

Clara shook her head and carried on walking, frustrated that she was allowing Isabella's jealousy to ruin her evening. "You were saying, Jack? About how she has turned a corner?"

"Yes, perhaps I was wrong on that front. That woman will probably never change, I—"

Just then, Jack and Clara heard a cry for help.

"Help! Help me!"

Jack looked around and saw Isabella lying on the frozen cobbles. "Quick, Clara, I think Isabella may have fallen."

Clara rolled her eyes. "She's probably being dramatic to get your attention."

"Clara, don't be so horrible, she's heavily pregnant, can't you see that?"

Jack ran towards the pregnant woman and Clara followed closely behind.

"Isabella, whatever happened?"

"I fell on the snow, ow! Please my baby, please help my baby."

Chapter 32

"It's okay, Isabella, everything will be okay," Clara was trying to soothe the pregnant woman so as not to panic her. She took her own coat off and put it over Isabella to keep her warm.

"I'm so sorry, Clara, for being horrible, I didn't mean it, I was just feeling hurt." She grabbed hold of Clara's hand tightly whilst talking through her tears.

"There, there, Isabella. Don't worry, the past doesn't matter". Clara looked at Jack and whispered to him. "Jack, can you run back to the Walker's house and fetch William and some blankets, I'm not sure of her husband's name."

"Yes, leave it with me, I should only be ten minutes." Jack ran as fast as he could back to the Walkers.

"Isabella, you have to be brave for yourself and strong for that beautiful baby of yours. When is it due?"

"In three weeks."

"That's good, at least you won't be too early, and how beautiful to have a Christmas baby if it is three weeks early? Nothing is a greater gift at Christmas time." Clara's hands wrapped around Isabella's and held them tightly. She looked up to the sky and saw the snow was starting to get heavy.

Isabella looked at Clara for reassurance whilst Jack ran for help.

Bang, bang, bang. Jack slammed the heavy iron door knocker three times. "Come on, William, where are you?"

Bang, bang ...

"Yes, yes, what is it? Jack! How are you, come in. I've not seen you in so long. There was no need for the persistence with the door knocks," William said with a smile.

"Please, William, you have to come with me quickly. Isabella has fallen on the snow, and she needs help. Clara is with her, but it's freezing outside and the snow is getting heavier."

William grabbed his coat.

"Quick, you will need a couple of blankets."

"Clarence! Come quickly!" William shouted up the stairs. "Clarence!"

"What is it?"

"Isabella had a fall in the snow."

"Clarence?" Jack said.

"Isabella's husband."

"I know who he is William, I suppose I shouldn't be surprised."

"They got married ten months ago. Here, grab this," William said, throwing a blanket at Jack distracting him from his thoughts.

Clarence took his slippers off, almost losing balance, and slipped his shoes on without undoing the laces.

The night sky had turned cloudy, and the snow began to fall. The three men ran as quickly as possible with the blankets towards the two ladies, snowflakes starting to show in their hair under the moonlight.

"What was she doing? I warned her about going out tonight."

"She needed air, Clarence, it's tough when you're pregnant and hard to get comfortable so late on. Charlotte had a terrible time when she was in the late stages of pregnancy, she was completely restless."

Clara could see the figures running towards them and sliding in the snow every time they hit a patch that had hardened on the ground.

"Oh, my love, I'm here for you now." Clarence ran up to his wife and skidded to a halt, falling to his knees. He put his arm under his wife's neck and cradled her in his arms.

"I'm sorry, Clarence. I didn't listen to you and went for a walk by myself. Now, see what has happened. I have put both mine and the baby's life in jeopardy."

"Don't be silly, everything will be just fine."

"I've tried to reassure her," Clara said as she held Isabella's hand whilst William covered her with blankets.

"Isabella, are you getting any pains anywhere?"

"No, William, it's just so sore and I think I can feel a contraction coming on."

"We need to get her up and home quickly," William whispered to Jack. "She can't have the child here. They will both freeze to death."

"Isabella, we need to get you up. Clarence and I will take opposite sides, no need to worry."

William and Clarence carefully lifted Isabella off the ground.

"Please let our baby be okay, Clarence, please."

"Let's get you home where it's warm, the baby will be fine."

"Jack, do you think you could run ahead for the doctor? It will be at least one hour if we are lucky before he could come to help" William tried to talk quietly so Isabella wouldn't panic.

Jack ran ahead whilst Clara stayed to reassure her. "You are doing fine, let's get you and that beautiful baby back safely, shall we?"

With every step, Isabella winced with pain from the contractions. The urge to push became more frequent with each foot forward. The cold snow made walking harder, and the journey seemed twice as long. Yet somehow, the warm, orange glow from the lights in the windows comforted the worried foursome as they stumbled their way back home.

As soon as they reached the Walker's house, Jack was waiting with more blankets and a bowl of warm water.

"Please, I don't think I can go any further," Isabella said as she sat down quickly on the entrance hall floor. Clarence and William caught her before she landed too hard on the caustic tiles.

"The doctor may arrive in time for the birth, or he may not."

"What did you say, Jack? No doctor?" Isabella was now crying with panic.

"Don't you worry, Isabella, I am here. William, Jack, you had best leave us whilst Isabella is in labour. You shouldn't be around."

William and Jack waited anxiously in the study, enjoying their whisky and the warm feeling it brought. William put his glass on the side table and added more coals and logs to the fire. This will be needed for the next few hours."

"How long until, you know?" Jack asked.

"I don't know. Charlotte's labours were both different. It could be in a few hours or anytime—"

William's sentence was interrupted by the baby's cries which echoed throughout the downstairs of the house. The noise broke the stillness of the room.

"It's a girl!" Clarence appeared at the door of the study with blood on his hands.

William and Jack ran into the entrance hall and skidded to a halt to witness Isabella sitting against the wall covered in blankets and holding her child.

"Oh, Clarence. Our Christmas baby. Isn't she beautiful? What shall we call her?"

"Let's call her Imogen Jane." A tribute to your grandmother.

Clarence looked at Clara and nodded once. *Thank you*, he mouthed, followed by a smile.

"It sounds perfect."

The fire crackled in the study as everyone gathered around mother and child. The large Christmas tree, which was standing against the banister of the stairs, was illuminated in the background. It truly was the perfect Christmas.

There was a sudden knock on the door.

"I see you have already given birth," Doctor Gargrieve said as he entered the house. "Let's check you over, shall we?"

The doctor gave his nod of approval and declared both mother and child healthy.

"Who helped with the birth?"

"Erm, I did, doctor." Clara said whilst looking adoringly at the child.

"Well done miss, you have done an excellent job."

"Here, would you like to hold her?"

Isabella passed the baby to Clara, and she held the bundle tightly so as not to drop her. Clara cradled Imogen in her arms.

"It suits you," Jack whispered in her ear.

"This doesn't mean you are getting out of performing, Jack. We may have missed the show tonight, but I'm not finished with you yet."

"I need to talk to you urgently about something before Jack comes downstairs."

"What would that be?"

"I think Jack will propose to me soon and ask for my hand in marriage."

"That's fabulous news, Clara. I'm so pleased for you. I know you are very fond of him."

"I am, but I want you to say no."

George placed his spoon in his bowl of porridge and looked at his daughter. "Why? I thought it's all you've ever wanted. A loving husband so you can have a family together and build happy memories."

"I want to marry Jack more than anything. But there are a couple of things. I want to get married at Christmas, so that means waiting another year."

"I'm flexible about the wedding date, Clara. No rush on my account. What was the other thing?"

"As you and I both know, Jack has a fabulous singing voice. Leo, the Adelphi Theatre manager, agrees. He has repeatedly asked Jack to audition for the upcoming production, but Jack refuses."

"So you keep saying. But you can't turn down a marriage proposal because he doesn't want to audition."

"Papa, you said he needs to try harder to find better work." You don't want your daughter to marry a man who is less than himself, do you?"

"I suppose not. I get it, and I want only the best for you," George smiled. He picked up his spoon and continued eating the warm bowl of oats and milk.

"Papa, I'm being serious. Don't smirk at me like that."

George let out a small sigh. "And so am I, Clara. He deserves to be on the stage, and we both know it. But are you going to let that stop you from marrying him? I expected you to have a different outlook on life after what happened with your mother. Don't go too hard on him."

"But I know it's his passion, he just needs a bit of a push. So, I'm going to have a word with Leo and ask him if Jack can sing at his house on New Year's Eve."

"How will you contact him?"

"I have it all planned out. Leo will pick up two suits in the shop the day after tomorrow. I will speak to him then."

George raised his eyebrows. "Fair enough. But what does that have to do with me?"

"I don't want you to give Jack permission to marry me until he earns a good wage, and that involves the theatre. I don't care how you go about it. I just need your help. Shh, he's coming."

"Morning!"

"Good morning, Jack, we were just talking about you and—"

Clara threw her father a look of discontent.

"About you and Christmas Jack, and how you seem to love it so much."

"I do. Even more so with you by my side. Which reminds me, George, can I speak to you after breakfast privately?"

George looked to Clara for guidance in the conversation. He was met with a blank look.

"Is it about anything in particular? Nothing too serious I hope, it is Christmas after all."

Clara quickly changed the subject of the conversation. "The Walkers will be celebrating with the birth of Imogen too. It will be a very happy Christmas for them."

"Yes, and they have such a joyful bundle. Maybe we'll be like that someday," Jack said, tucking a serviette into his collar.

The room fell silent. Jack's knees shook under the table and he looked at Clara.

"Right, well obviously you two would like to talk so I will make myself scarce, shall I?" Clara stood up from the table and wandered off towards the library to read, but stopped just the other side of the door to the breakfast room. She cupped a hand against her ear and leaned against the door.

"As you know I am very fond of your daughter. She is amazing and I want to spend my life with her."

"It would be marvelous to have you in the family Jack, I have known you a long time and admire your courage. I think you would be perfect for Clara."

What is my father saying? I told him not to give his permission! Clara listened nervously and hoped her father would go along with her plan.

"Oh right, well thank you. In which case, I was wondering if you would give me your permission to marry Clara?"

"No."

"No? But I thought you said it would be marvelous to have me."

"Indeed, it would be, Jack. But not just yet."

Yes! Clara smiled and bit her bottom lip. She brought her ear back closer to the door.

"When then? I know we are still quite young, but I promise to look after her."

"Oh, Jack, dear boy, it has nothing to do with that. You are perfect for Clara, but there are a couple of things that might get in the way. Clara wants to get married at Christmas, so you'll have to wait."

"I will wait for her. But what is the second thing?"

"The thing is Jack, I know you are working at your uncle's shop, but is it enough for you? Will you be able to sustain a good enough income for my daughter and your future family? You know how Clara has very high expectations for an abundant lifestyle. And her mother's inheritance will not last forever the speed at which she is spending it."

My cheeky father! I don't spend that much, do I?

"I would have thought my income would be fine."

"Fine, yes. Exceptional, no. Jack, you are capable of much more! Have you considered pursuing theatre with your magnificent voice?"

"Has Clara been talking to you?"

"She mentioned that you have a talent, and I've heard it since you were a young boy. But you have turned down many auditions offered by Mr Cooper."

"Ah, yes, Mr Cooper. The thing is, I'm just not confident enough, and I thought Clara was happy for me to continue working at my uncle's tailors." Jack picked up his coffee cup and slurped the last of the dregs. A habit he hadn't grown out of.

"She is, Jack, if that's what you want. If you truly want to marry my daughter, you may need to reconsider. I will leave you to ponder and see you at dinner."

George walked out leaving Jack in the breakfast room. "Good grief, Clara, you nearly made me jump out of my skin," George whispered. "You weren't listening in, were you?"

"Who me? No, of course not."

Chapter 33

"**W**here were you? I waited all night, but you never showed up."

"I'm so sorry, Leo. Would you believe we got caught up in an emergency? We were on our way to see the show, but a friend went into early labour in the snow."

"That sounds a little dramatic, you could make that into a Christmas story."

"You are always so full of ideas Leo. Anyway, the fact is, we missed seeing Nancy. We were so disappointed."

"I suppose Jack was pleased wasn't he?"

"Well, I think he thought he'd avoided it."

"How will you persuade him to audition?"

"I do not know. That was our one chance for him to meet Nancy. I was hoping she would have talked him around."

"There is another idea."

"What's that?" Clara said as she packaged Leo's suits for him.

"Nancy and her husband Percy are having a New Year's Eve celebration. The singer providing the entertainment has pulled out. Diphtheria apparently, dreadful disease."

Clara had a flashback to when her mother died and her eyes began to water. It was the first time she had felt saddened by her mother's death.

"Are you okay, Clara? You've gone quiet."

Clara shook her thoughts away out of her mind. "Yes, yes, I'm fine. What does that have to do with Jack?"

"Do you have any plans for the evening?"

"No, none that I can think of anyway," she said whilst taking payment for Leo's suits.

"In which case, how about you, Jack, and your father come to Nancy and Percy's house? I will speak to them and let them know what's happening. We could get Jack there on the pretence that it's a New Year celebration. Then we can tell him that the singer pulled out last minute. I'm sure he would sing for us wouldn't he?"

"Well, impromptu is better because he gets nervous. Knowing at the last minute won't give him the chance to refuse."

"Great, I will see you all tomorrow evening. Jack has a fine voice you know. It's a talent wasted here in this shop. No disrespect to you or Mr Dalton. It's just that we all have talents, but many go to waste because people end up doing something that doesn't fulfil them. The next production starts in March, I wonder if we could persuade him?"

"My father and I have decided Jack needs a gentle push and my father has almost made it a condition that he sings before he can marry me."

"Sounds like he just needs a bit of help. How do we convince him to audition for the show?"

"Leave that part to me, Leo. All you need to do is admire his singing on New Year's Eve and tell him how good he is. Father and I will back you up. Then you can ask him again to audition, maybe Nancy would help too. I'm quite sure he will say yes now father has spoken to him about it."

"I am still searching for the leading man in The Shaughran. It's Nancy's opening show for next year and it will sell out."

"I would love Jack to star in that."

"In which case, I will see you at seven o'clock. Here is the address." Leo scribbled Nancy and Percy's address on a piece of paper and passed it to Clara.

"Thanks, Leo, you won't regret this," Clara said, taking the address from Leo and putting it in her intricately embroidered carpet bag.

"I'm sure I won't," he said, leaving with the suits perfectly wrapped.

Chapter 34

The carriage wheels rolled along the cobbles through Holly Village. Despite Christmas being over, windows still displayed Christmas trees and decorations, while snowflakes covered holly bushes on doorsteps.

Clara looked at Jack who was sitting opposite her in the carriage, her father sat to the side. Jack's eyes widened in delight at the surrounding sights.

"You do love Christmas, don't you, Jack?"

"I do, Clara, and I know you want to get married at Christmas time. I'm not surprised with it being a magical time of year."

"I hope Nancy and Percy still have their tree decorated."

"You sound like you know them personally, calling them by their first names."

"I suppose Leo has spoken that much about them, I feel as if I do."

"Tell me again, why did they invite us?" I would have thought we would have no place at their New Year's Eve celebration. We have never met them before."

"Leo was kind, inviting us, Jack. We have got to know him and he considers us friends."

"Yes, I agree. But it's not his house, is it? So why did he invite us?"

Jack was right, why would Leo invite them to someone else's house on New Year's Eve? She had to think quickly so Jack wouldn't suspect a thing.

"Leo was meant to have the celebration at his house. But he decided it was too small for the number of invites sent. So Nancy and Percy agreed to have it at their home. Nancy is Leo's best friend, so I wouldn't consider it unusual that she would invite Leo's friends to help bring in the New Year and carry out the first-footing."

"I suppose not."

George looked sideways at his daughter, and Clara let out a silent breath of relief.

The carriage slowed to a stop outside Nancy's and Percy's house.

"Here you are, miss," said the groomsman. He stepped down when the horses brought the carriage to a halt, then he opened the door for everyone to step out. "Watch how you go now. I will be waiting right here to take you back."

"Thank you, Giles. The house staff have said you are more than welcome to join them in the kitchen near the fire and drink warm tea whilst you wait."

"Thank you, miss, I will do that."

Clara, her father, Jack, and Cecil walked up the steps whilst admiring the entrance. They knocked on the ornamental front door, which was framed in a wreath of holly and berries, and were greeted by the butler. "Please come this way. The hosts are waiting for you."

Jack followed Nancy, George, and Cecil through to the drawing room. Clara looked over her shoulder and noticed him slip back and slow down. She stopped and allowed her father and Cecil to go ahead. "Come on Jack, you will be just fine. I know there are a lot of people, but you are with us. You have nothing to be nervous about."

Jack walked into the drawing room and noticed the lid on the grand piano was open. The stool was set back from the keys as if waiting for the pianist to fill the seat.

"Clara, Cecil, Jack, how good it is to see you all! And this must be your father, George. It's wonderful to meet you Mr Cavendish, I've heard a lot about you."

"I hope it's all been good, Leo, and my daughter hasn't been blackening my name," he said with a smile.

"I've heard nothing but good things about you."

"That's good to hear."

"Leo! Why don't you introduce us?" Nancy said as she walked over to her best friend. The champagne in her glass sparkled against the lights, the bubbles floating in the gold-coloured liquid. "This is Jack, the singer, I keep telling you about him."

"So you're our stand in entertainer for this evening," Nancy said, holding her hand out to shake Jack's. It's good to meet you at last. Leo tells me you have a powerful voice."

"Stand in entertainer? Nobody told me about that?" Jack looked at Clara. "Did you have anything to do with this?"

"Excuse me, I must go and powder my nose." Clara swiftly left the room, leaving Leo to explain what had happened.

"She's not entirely to blame, Jack. I agreed to it when she asked. All in the name of helping you onto the stage."

"But Leo, I told her I wasn't ready!"

"Jack, listen to me," Nancy said, putting on her best warm smile. "You have nothing to be nervous about. If what Leo says is true, you will be better than the entertainer we hired anyway. Simply follow the music and sing along."

"I—I'm sorry, I can't do it." Jack rubbed the back of his neck and beads of sweat formed on his brow. His eyes wandered around the room. The strangers, drinking and being merry, stared back at him. A hundred eyes were upon him.

"Jack you're sweating, are you okay?" Cecil put a loving hand on his shoulder.

"No, no, I'm not. This is too much, I'm sorry." He shoved the glass of champagne they gave him on arrival towards George, who had no choice but to take the glass from him.

"Jack! Where are you going? Everybody is waiting!"

Jack ran out of the drawing room, eyes watched in surprise as he ran towards the front door and onto the street.

"Where's Jack gone?" Clara said when she came back from reapplying the red salve to her cheeks and lips.

"Looks like your man has changed his mind. Shame, I was looking forward to hearing him sing. There could have been an audition opportunity for him."

"I'm sorry, Nancy, how rude. Let me find him," Clara said.

"I think you're too late. He went out the front door."

Clara picked up the trusses of her skirt, turned around, and chased after her darling.

"It's a shame," George said. "Clara has made it quite clear she won't marry him unless he performs on the stage. She wants a rising star for a husband and what my daughter wants, she always gets."

"I wouldn't be so sure about that. Jack left quickly. It's like he didn't want to be caught by anyone," Cecil responded.

"Jack! Jack!" Clara ran down the steps and onto the street. Jack ran ahead, disappearing from sight when he turned a corner.

"Jack! Jack!" Her voice echoed in the darkness, unheard by anyone.

Chapter 35

⚜

C lara stopped and leaned over. Her hands balanced on her knees and she tried to catch her breath. Her chest hurt so much through exertion, she was almost sick. "Jack! Jack!" she whispered. "Please, don't go." She gazed towards the ground, then closed her eyes, and prayed she hadn't lost her one true love for good.

Clara stood up straight, put her hands on her hips and looked ahead. There was still no sign of him. She started walking towards where she last saw her sweetheart running. As she reached the corner, she felt a hand on her shoulder. Clara yelped a little, her heart racing through the fright of who it could be. She spun around quickly and almost burst into tears. "Jack!" she said, thumping his chest then allowing her head to rest against him. "I thought you were gone."

"Shh, I'm here. I'm sorry." He stroked her hair and kissed the top of her head. "I'm so sorry for running, I was being foolish. I allowed my nerves to get the better of me."

Clara moved her head backwards away from his chest. "You scared me, Jack. I thought you wouldn't come back. Oh, Jack. I'm sorry for what I did. I never meant to put you under pressure."

"Please don't apologise, it was my stupid fault. And now I feel embarrassed. You've gone to all that trouble to make sure I pursue my dreams, and all I can do is throw it back in your face. Please forgive me."

"Of course. You are my everything. I should never have done it. Why don't we just go home?"

Jack fell silent for a moment. He considered Clara's invitation and his eyes began to water. Her honesty of admitting she was wrong made him fall in love with her even more. If that was possible.

Jack looked up and down at Clara. "No."

"No? What do you mean?" Clara's heart thumped in her chest, her stomach feeling uneasy from his stern response.

"No, we're not going home. You look beautiful tonight, It's New Year's Eve, and I'm not going to allow my ego to ruin it for you. Let's go back and join everyone. I'm sure I will be able to overcome my embarrassment of running away."

"But, Jack. It doesn't matter. I don't expect you to go back there. No one will notice us missing."

"Yes they will. And besides, I know how much Christmas means to you after what happened to your mother. I won't ruin this for you like she did. I'm so sorry for being selfish, your happiness means everything to me, I just didn't think." Jack wrapped his arms around his love, never wanting to let go.

"I love you so much, Jack."

"And I, you, Clara." Jack took her by the hand, squeezed it tight, and led her back to the celebrations through the falling snowflakes.

"Jack! Clara! We didn't think you would come back, did we, George?" Cecil said. "I for one am glad you are here."

"Look at me. My hair is bedraggled and I feel a mess."

"You are still beautiful to me, Clara."

George and Cecil smiled at the young couple, and the butler walked over with fresh champagne.

"Did I hear someone say they look bedraggled? We can't have that on New Year's Eve, can we?" Nancy seemingly had appeared from nowhere. "Jessica? Take Clara to get cleaned up. I'm sure she will feel much better when you have helped her tidy herself up."

"Thank you, Nancy, I didn't expect that."

"It's my pleasure." As Nancy watched her maid take Clara to freshen up, she spoke to Jack. "You need to overcome your nerves, Jack, if you are ever going to perform."

"I know, I'm sorry. It's been a long time since I sang in front of a big crowd. Maybe it's because my pa always laughed at me and told me to stop being a wussy." Jack's eyes glazed over.

"Well that won't have helped." Nancy touched Jack's forearm. "You will be fine, I promise. Come with me."

Nancy led Jack to the front of the room and stood by the piano. "Now then. This young man 'ere is a bit nervous. He's been asked to perform at short notice, but his shyness gets the better of him. So if we're all going to have a good night into the early hours, I suggest we give him our support. "'Ere," Nancy said, passing Jack a crystal low ball of brandy. Have a gulp of this and sing to your 'earts content me lad."

Jack raised his glass, knocked the drink back in one, and opened his mouth. He urged his voice to fill the room with gentle notes as the whole room was quiet, waiting expectantly. But nothing came out.

Nancy looked at him and nodded encouragingly. "Why don't I help?" The star whispered. She moved closer to him and started singing.

As Jack duetted with Nancy Franklin, the biggest star on the London show scene, he caught his love's eyes at the back of the room.

Clara tentatively stepped inside the drawing room having wondered where the singing was coming from. She slowly made her way through the room full of festive invitees. People moved out of her way and allowed her to the front. And there, at the front of the room, as she watched Jack and Nancy sing together, she cried tears of happiness.

Chapter 36

One Year Later

C lara, George, Cecil, Clarence, and the Walkers had a private box on the right side of the stage. They were excited to see Jack perform. The production had five-star reviews from journalists and tickets had sold out. Chances of getting a ticket were slim. Unless, of course, you were willing to queue at the box office for hours in the rain, or you were related to one of the performers. Imogen had been left with the nanny at George's house, giving Clara a night off from child care.

"Are you excited, Clarence? I know it's a difficult time of year for you and it's your first Christmas since having Imogen and, without Isabelle here."

"Clara, you and Jack have been marvelous in helping me bring up Imogen. Truly, Isabella would not have wanted anybody else to care for our child."

"Still, you must be feeling her absence, particularly at this time of year. It's Imogen's first real Christmas. It must be hard for you."

"I miss her terribly. But I also know that she is watching over us. Her death was too soon, but she lives on in our beautiful daughter."

The lights went down, the curtain was raised, and the theatre became silent. As the orchestra played, Jack emerged from the side of the stage and began singing.

"Clara, shh. Jack's on."

Clara picked up her theatre binoculars and looked at her beloved below. It had been mainly Clara's doing to get Jack to audition, a plan that was perfectly executed. And now Jack and Clara were to be married on Christmas Eve. Clara's winter miracle was finally coming true.

"Bravo! Bravo! Bravo!"

The audience stood and cheered at the end of the opening night's performance. Jack had become well known at the Cambridge Hartman Theatre thanks to Nancy. No one could have anticipated how big a star Jack would become.

"It's such a shame that Jack's mother could not be here to see her son perform."

"Yes, Clara, I agree. But she will be happy knowing that he found me."

As the audience started to leave and walk into the winter snow outside, Clara waited for Jack to join them.

"Oh, Jack, my love, you were fantastic."

"Thank you, Clara," Jack said, blushing. Despite lacking confidence, I can now perform without rushing to the closet before the curtain rises."

"Shall we head back to the house everybody? We have a big day coming up."

Clara, Jack, George, and Cecil rode together in the carriage back to Holly village.

It was ten o'clock by the time they arrived at home, having ridden through the streets with the snow falling and spotting Christmas trees in windows.

"Oh, Jack, isn't this just beautiful? It's Christmas time and snowing and we have Imogen to return home to. Life is perfect as we are about to marry."

This will be our best Christmas ever, I know it."

"It certainly is Jack."

"We've arrived miss", Giles said as he helped Clara down from the carriage."

As they stepped into the house, Cecil made an announcement.

"Would you mind all joining me for a small drink before we retire? I have something to say and want to make the most of the wonderful feelings we have from the evening."

"Oh, this is exciting, Cecil, I wonder what you are going to reveal."

The nanny informed Clara and Jack in the drawing room that Imogen was peacefully sleeping in the nursery. "I started up your music box miss. Sent the young lass to sleep straight away."

"Thank you, Florence." Clara had given Imogen the music box her father had bought her all those years ago. It soothed and calmed Imogen as it had Clara when she was a young girl.

"Now then, let's have a toast, shall we?" Cecil raised his glass. "To Jack and Clara."

"To Jack and Clara!" Everyone joined in.

"And I must add," Cecil continued, "It's a joy for Jack to be in my life and marrying Clara tomorrow."

"Here, here!" George said, taking a sip of his brandy. "I'm thrilled for both of you."

"And there is something else." Cecil reached inside his jacket and pulled out a small box. "Your mother left me something, Jack. Something I know that she would want your wife to cherish. Pass it on to your children when the time is right."

Cecil passed the small box to Jack. As Jack put his drink down, he looked at his uncle with anticipation. He opened the lid to reveal a beautiful emerald and gold ring. The green, oval stone was set in gold, with three smaller square diamonds either side. The precious stones shone brightly under the lights.

"Uncle, I remember this."

"Beautiful isn't it? She had left it to me after she died. Your father may have beaten her black and blue, but he made sure that I passed this to you. Your parents loved you, Jack."

Jack kneeled down in front of Clara with a tear in his eye. He took hold of Clara's right hand and put the ring on her fourth finger.

"Happy Christmas, my love, from my parents and I to you."

"Thank you so much, I will treasure it forever until it is passed on to our children."

Clara hugged Jack and everyone raised their glasses.

"Ma and pa," Jack toasted proudly, beaming at his wife-to-be.

Epilogue

C hristmas Eve arrived, and the ground had a crisp layer of pure white snow. The red berries peeked between the green leaves and pure white snowflakes, were bright on the holly bushes, and the Poinsettia plants lined the driveway to the house. Inside George and Clara's home, the staircase adorned a beautiful green and red garland. The frames on the walls had sprigs of holly along the top, and greenery wreaths hung from the internal doors.

Candles were lit in the windows, and the house was spotless. Staff busied themselves in the kitchen, and the gardener cleared the snow away from the drive.

Jack and Cecil had both stayed at Clara and George's house the entire week before the wedding. It had been a busy affair, with the week before Christmas in full swing, dinners, music, and celebrations.

"Oh, Jack, I'm so very pleased we found each other."

"Same here, uncle, and thank you for being my best man today."

"Jack, I feel honoured to be by your side, you know your mother and father would have been proud, don't you?"

"I'm not so sure about my pa, but my ma will be watching over me."

"Don't be so sure about your pa, Jack. He and your ma had their differences, but—"

"Differences?" Jack cut in and tutted. "That's putting it mildly."

Cecil flapped his hand slightly in the air in front of him. "Just hear me out, Jack. I want you to have a good impression of your pa and remember him fondly. He and your ma may have had their differences, but he always loved you. Your ma put in her letter that he searched for you for weeks after you left. He wouldn't have done that if he didn't love you."

"I suppose you're right," he sighed. "But I still can't forgive him for what he did."

"You don't have to. He loved you and would be proud."

Jack walked over to his uncle and embraced him. "Thank you, I don't know what I would do without you. You are like a grandpa to little Imogen now, too. It was unpredictable what had happened to Isabella.

"Imogen couldn't be in better hands. You and Clara are perfect for looking after her. And no doubt you will be having your own children soon, too."

"I hope so. And maybe you could be their godfather."

"I would love that, Jack, thank you. I've never had children of my own and feel I've missed out. What are the plans for the theatre after the wedding?"

"There are productions running throughout the year, so it looks like I will be busy. Clara is going to travel around with me. We can be together all the time and she wants to bring Imogen with us as well."

"Is that wise?"

"We are fortunate to have the money to bring the nanny. Clara has always wanted to travel around London. Now we can do it together."

"It sounds perfect. I'll always be here to support you, Jack. But we need to leave. Let's go and meet George downstairs."

"You do look smart, Jack," George said, waiting at the bottom of the stairs.

"Thank you, George, as do you. Any sign of the bride yet?"

"No, not yet. I expect she is taking her time getting ready. I know that her maid is up there helping her into her wedding gown."

"I for one cannot wait to see her."

"Jack, I think we should make our way to the church, don't you? You can't see the bride just yet, it's bad luck."

"Jack just before you go—" George walked over to his future son-in-law. I'm proud of the person you've become, overcoming your struggles and performing in the theatre. I know it couldn't have been easy for you without your parents. I'm truly delighted Clara is marrying you.

"Thank you, George, for accepting me into your house and allowing me to marry your daughter."

"Father, is it safe to come downstairs?" Clara shouted.

"Quick, Jack, we must go. George, I shall see you at the church," Cecil said as he rushed his nephew out of the house and into the carriage which was waiting for him.

Clara had no bridesmaids except for Imogen, who was to travel to the church with her and George. The nanny had taken Imogen from Clarence an hour before so she could dress her ready for the wedding.

"Clara, you look beautiful, darling."

"Thank you. I didn't think it was right to wear my mother's wedding gown, so I had this made by Cecil."

"I wouldn't have had anybody else make it for you, it's perfect isn't it?"

Clara slowly made her way downstairs in her wedding gown made from pure silk with a frame and layers of tulle underneath the skirt. The bodice was fitted with intricate pearl detail, buttons down the back, and a six-foot train. "You only get married once. I wanted it to be special."

"Nothing is too special for my daughter."

"Mama, Mama."

"Oh, there you are, darling. Thank you, Florence, I will take Imogen from here. I will see you after the wedding."

Clara and George stepped into the carriage. Florence passed Imogen to Clara, along with a bouquet of deep red roses. Imogen had hold of a basket of rose petals that were spilling over the top as the young child swung it freely from side to side.

"It's a good job I have a spare, I'm not sure a basket was the best idea for a one-year-old."

Clara looked at Imogen and felt blessed. She had a daughter she could cherish and love with all of her heart.

"Off to the church we go," she said, bouncing the child on her hip.

Clara anticipated there would be a day when she and Jack would have to explain to Imogen about her birth mother and why her father entrusted them with her care.

She hoped that by showing love and care, Imogen would still want to live with them. After all, Clara believed that when love prevailed, anything was possible.

But for now, she was consumed by thoughts of her special day ahead. A daughter's dreams of a winter miracle, which had come true without her mother's love. Thinking about it too deeply would hurt and bruise her precious heart.

Clara kissed Imogen on her cheek and smiled. Then she gazed out of the window as the carriage wheels rolled along the snow-lined street. She smiled as she silently promised herself that the painful memories would be erased from her mind from this day forward.

THE END

About the Author

If you enjoyed The Daughter's Winter Miracle, the second book in the series ***The Starlet Slum Girl*** is now available to download here: https://mybook.to/TheStarletSlumGirl

My free book, ***The Whitechapel Angel***, is also available for download here: https://dl.bookfunnel.com/xs5p4d0oog

My next book, ***The Lost Girl's Miracle***, is due to be released on 29th March 2024.

About the Author:

I have always been passionate about historical romance set in the Victorian era. I love to place myself on the dark, murky streets of London and wonder what it would have been like to overcome tragedy and poverty to find true love. The different classes of society intrigue me and I'm fascinated to know if love ever truly prevailed between the working and upper class.

I'm not sure about you, but whenever I visit the streets of Whitechapel, or read historical books from the bygone era, I find myself transported back to a time when I once lived there myself. Some say past lives are a myth, past life transgression is a 'load of tosh,' and you only ever live this life in the now. But whether you believe in past lives or not, for me, I easily feel myself living in those times.

With each book, I strive to create stories that capture the heart and imagination of my readers, bringing to life the strong, resilient characters that live in that bygone era.

When not writing, I can be found exploring the great outdoors with my husband Mike, and my Jack Russell, Daisy, or curled up with a good book. There is nothing quite like lighting the log burner and a candle or two, and turning the pages.

Stay connected:

Please, if you have any feedback, email me at <u>anneliesemmckay@gmail.com</u> (my admin assistant,) and I will respond to all of you personally.

Printed in Great Britain
by Amazon

38565810R00106